STARFELL

Willow Moss and the Vanished Kingdom

Books by Dominique Valente

STARFELL: WILLOW MOSS AND THE LOST DAY

STARFELL: WILLOW MOSS AND THE FORGOTTEN TALE

STARFELL: WILLOW MOSS AND THE VANISHED KINGDOM

STARFELL: WILLOW MOSS AND THE MAGIC THIEF

STARFELL

Willow Moss and the Vanished Kingdom

DOMINIQUE VALENTE

ILLUSTRATED BY SARAH WARBURTON

HarperCollins *Children's Books*

First published in Great Britain by
HarperCollins *Children's Books* in 2021
Published in this paperback edition 2022
HarperCollins *Children's Books* is a division of HarperCollins*Publishers* Ltd
HarperCollins Publishers
1 London Bridge Street
London SE1 9GF

www.harpercollins.co.uk

HarperCollins*Publishers*
1st Floor, Watermarque Building, Ringsend Road
Dublin 4, Ireland
1

HARDBACK ISBN 978-0-00-830847-6
TRADE PAPERBACK ISBN 978-0-00-837715-1
PAPERBACK ISBN 978-0-00-830848-3
SPECIAL EDITION ISBN 978-0-00-847916-9

A CIP catalogue record for this title is available from the British Library.

Printed and bound in the UK using 100% renewable electricity at CPI Group (UK) Ltd

MIX
Paper from
responsible sources
FSC™ C007454

This book is produced from independently certified FSC™ paper to ensure responsible forest management.

For more information visit: www.harpercollins.co.uk/green

For Rui, thank you for always
helping me find the magic

THE WEST
N
W
E
S
The Witch's Last Brew
The Old Winged Dragon
The Tree of Souls
The Troll's Lament
The Crooked Crown

THE EAST
The Old Hag
The Man who Lost his Shoe
The Big Dinner Party
The Wise Elf at the Bunfire
The Flight of Whispering Geese

The Grimoire Gazette

THE OFFICIAL ENCHANCIL NEWSLETTER REPORTING ON THE STATE OF MAGIC ACROSS THE WILDS OF STARFELL

Letter from the Editor

Well, chins have certainly been wagging about the appointment of the new leader of the Brothers of Wol, Silas Wolbrother! His leadership has kicked off with a radical new amendment to the treaty between magical and non-magical citizens – magical children below the age of thirteen will now be allowed to attend non-magical schools for the first time in Starfell's history.

Head of the Enchancil (Enchanted Council), Celestine Bear, believes that Silas's appointment as leader of the non-magical community will ensure a happier era for us all. In an exclusive interview (*page two*), she says, 'Look at what Silas has achieved in such a short time. Admittedly, it's not something we magical folk ever actually asked for, so it's a total surprise, but what a win! Who knows? One day we may even be able to convince the Brothers that a school of our own won't result in them being blown to smithereens. It's just so promising!'

However, our notorious twelve-year-old correspondent,

Willow Moss, disagrees. *Gazette* readers will no doubt be familiar with the young witch's wild stories – for example, her accusation that the very same new High Master 'stole a day' (which, conveniently, no one can remember).

'Silas cannot be trusted. The Enchancil have been tricked by him somehow,' she claims, adding that he is 'actually a wizard – who wants to steal everyone's magic'. Apparently, Willow discovered Silas's 'diabolical plan' while on a trip to the realm of the undead a few months ago.

'Clearly, young Willow has lost the plot,' counters Bear. 'Everyone knows that it is impossible to simply "visit" Netherfell – unless you want to lose your soul! The girl is delusional.'

However, some Enchancil members were concerned by Willow's claims – as she was backed by the infamous and powerful witch, Moreg Vaine. At Moreg's request, Willow was allowed to address the Enchancil with her latest tale some months back, despite being underage, and she has been sending the *Gazette* a steady stream of letters about it ever since.

Yet fears died down quickly after Moreg went silent on the issue. In fact, she has been missing in action for the past three months.

Bear adds, 'Thankfully, sense seems to have prevailed and most now agree that this rumour about Silas boils down to the fact that Willow is either rather unwell or has a desperate need for attention. The fact that Moreg has sloped off – well, that should speak for itself. She's probably embarrassed that she was ever taken in, if you ask me.' *More on pages three, four and seven, and find Willow's latest outrageous letter on page nine.*

Another occurrence that has got lips flapping this week is a clash between the elvish city of Lael and the town of Library, as a priceless scroll has been stolen from the bookish town. Many elves believe that the scroll contains the location of the vanished elvish kingdom of Llandunia, which disappeared, along with Queen Almefeira, during the Long War.

However, most Library historians believe that this is just a myth, as no one has been able to decipher the scroll in over a thousand years. 'It could be something as boring as an old elvish recipe for bread,' said one of the Secret Keepers, Copernica Darling, when pressed. 'Still, it is an ancient, unique artefact and that makes it very valuable. We are offering a reward for its safe return.' *More on page ten.*

Speaking of strange thefts, there has been a string

of these recently. Towns around the Midnight Market, Lael and Howling have fallen victim to burglary – including my own home, though the only thing taken was an old eyeball I was saving for a rainy day. Enchancil enforcers believe that the suspects could be linked to a group of pirate-wizards who are trying to reclaim the Ditchwater district within the city of Beady Hill, which was granted Forbidden status earlier this year . . . *More on this on page eleven.*

Finally, in Troll Country (*see our double-page spread on pages twelve and thirteen*), new attempts to expand Troll territory into Dwarfish lands have been met with resistance.

Magnus Pack, a spokesdwarf, says, 'We will not give so much as an extra toehold to those flat-footed monsters. To see our beloved forests trampled by their clubs and heavy feet? They must be mad.'

Troll chief Megrat hurled a studded club at me when I asked for a comment. I was given to understand by her daughter, Calamity, that this meant I should run, so I did.

Rubix Grimoire

Editor-in-chief

The hare was a scrawny thing with long limbs, patchy grey fur and an ear that looked like it had endured some chewing.

It was perfectly ordinary, apart from the fact that it was glowing faintly blue and was, in fact, a ghost.

The witch kept a watchful gaze pinned on it as it followed after her from a distance.

Then she reached inside the pocket of her new portal cloak and, after a bit of rummaging, took out a bed roll, a cheese sandwich and a rolled-up newspaper. She was saving the crossword for later.

It would be some time before she knew again the full comforts of home . . . For now, there was business to do – a witch's business, which is always her own.

Up above the purple marshes, the sky had turned to pewter, and the part of herself that had taken a moment to listen to the song of a passing sparrow heard a storm begin to brew. One that had little to do with the weather.

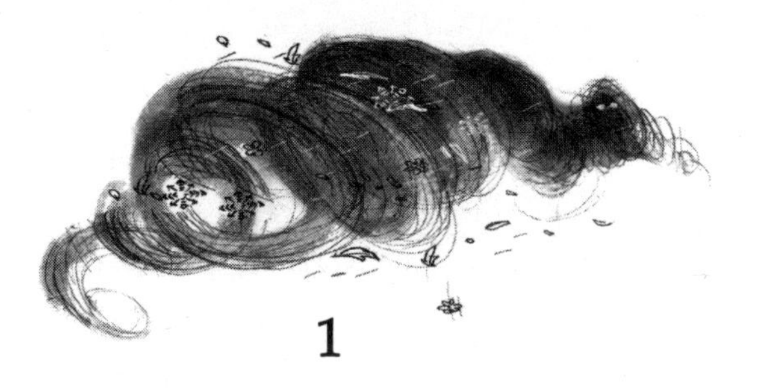

1

A Blundering Beginning

In a blister of a village called Mild, where the sun was hunkering down for a sulk, Willow Moss was having a bad day.

See, it was her first day at a new school – a school that was governed by the Brothers of Wol. And, while first days at a new school are always a bit tough, Willow's seemed destined to set the record for Worst Day Ever and, with the day being young, there was always the chance that things could actually get *worse.*

As far as thoughts went, this wasn't exactly a comforting one. But that's the trouble with thoughts, you know? The bad ones grow like spiky weeds and, if you aren't careful to prune them, you'll be left with a mind full of thorns. And what Willow was thinking right then was that, if she could do it all over again,

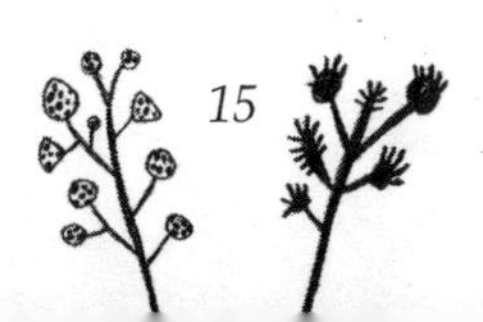

she would go about things a bit differently . . .

For instance, she might have reconsidered entering the school grounds on the back of a flying broomstick named Whisper . . .

She had realised this was a mistake rather quickly.

Thanks to the screaming . . .

. . . And the way the students scrambled to hide beneath their desks when she entered the classroom. There was also the boy in the corner making the sign of Wol at her as if to ward off evil. Then there was the fact that the teacher had flattened himself against the wall when she turned to him, arms raised above his head, as if Willow were a dangerous viper poised to strike.

Not exactly *ideal.*

The second thing she might have reconsidered was bringing along the monster from under the bed.

Oswin, the monster in question (and her best friend), chose that precise moment to pop his shaggy head out of the hairy green carpetbag she was carrying. His green, lamp-like eyes squinted in the daylight as he

harrumphed, **'WOT a bunch o' cumberworlds . . . Yew'd fink they'd never seen a witch afore. 'Tis not like yer gonna ketch 'em all an' turn 'em inter stew or sumfink . . .'** A low belly rumble followed this pronouncement, and he added, a little mournfully, **'Actuallys, I could jes *murder* a bowl of stew abouts now . . .'**

This, unfortunately, elicited more panicked wailings.

'It's a talking cat!'

'Why is that cat green?'

'Did it just say it wants to turn us into STEW?'

'Oh Wol, it's changing colour!'

'Oh, the smell! Oh, save us . . .'

And that sort of thing.

Willow fished out the StoryPass from her pocket. It was a compass-like device from the town of Library that was supposed to help with novel cataloguing, but offered useful life advice as well. The five points were:

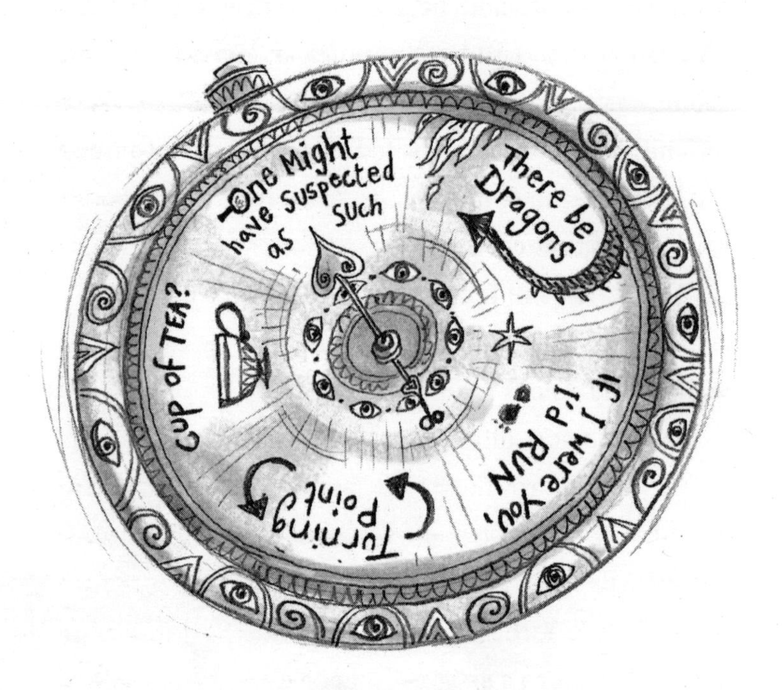

It was currently pointing to '*One Might Have Suspected as Such*'.

Willow sighed, then pushed Oswin's head – which had turned from the colour of pea soup to a violent blood-orange – back in the bag.

'I is not A CAT . . . I is the monster from under the bed! Honestly, wot do they teach kits in skewls nowadaisies?' he hissed.

'Just leave it,' Willow whispered, pinching the bridge of her nose.

There was a harrumph from Oswin – who was in fact a kobold, a subspecies of monster. Alas, he did look like a cat, but calling any attention to this resemblance made him rather upset – and this, in turn, made him change colour. Sometimes, if you upset him enough, he *blew up* . . . which would only make the situation worse.

This was not at all how Willow had hoped things would go today.

Before she'd left home that morning, Willow's father, Hawthorn, had given her a packed lunch that included two gumbo apples and a sandwich filled with eel-liver paste. It was one of those situations in which the phrase 'it's the thought that counts' was sure to apply. Hawthorn's almond-shaped eyes, which looked so much like Willow's, had sparkled.

'Oh, Willow,' he'd beamed. 'I still remember my years at school rather fondly, despite all the scars. It will be such fun to compare notes.'

Willow had felt momentarily uneasy as she nodded

and smiled. She did not enjoy lying to her family, pretending she had come round to the idea of attending school, but she could see no other choice.

Her wrist still ached from writing urgent letters about Silas to the *Grimoire Gazette* that were dismissed or ridiculed. The editor, Rubix Grimoire – once an ally, and the guardian of Willow's good friend Essential – had seemingly turned against Willow altogether. And Moreg Vaine, the one person who might have been able to persuade the Enchancil of the truth, was nowhere to be found. All of this had caused Willow more sleepless nights than she could count.

She was tired of being ignored. Tired of having no answers. She needed to find out for herself why the Brothers of Wol had suddenly changed their minds and allowed magical children into their schools . . . and why nobody else seemed confused by this reversal.

In her hairy green carpetbag, Willow had packed enough clothes and food to last for a few days, and she'd left a note in her bedroom telling her family she wasn't coming home until she'd got to the bottom of what was happening.

So a better, more well-thought-out plan might have been for her to try to *blend in* a bit more with

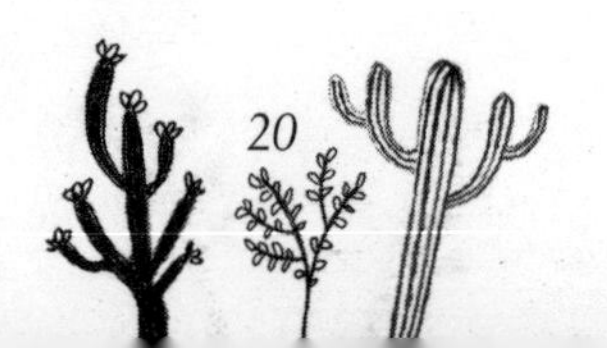

the non-magical children – to keep her head down and her eyes and ears open. Instead, she was standing out in a rather worrisome way. But Willow couldn't help thinking that Oswin had a point. The class's reaction to her was a little . . . puzzling.

The village of Mild was only about five miles away from Grinfog, where Willow's magical family lived, so she'd assumed they would've heard about her. Yet, considering most of the children's reactions, she might as well have come from somewhere as far away as Starfell's second moon, Hezelboob (which was said to have spun off several thousand miles away from its first moon, Jezelboob, many eons ago in the luminary equivalent of a family spat). Perhaps it was more than that, though – perhaps they *had* heard of her, but were still afraid?

Thankfully, a small handful of children from Grinfog were looking just as puzzled as Willow was by the panic. Willow recognised a boy with green eyes and dark brown skin named Peg Spoon, who she often saw down by the river, fishing. He shot some of the others a bemused look before giving Willow a small wave, which she returned.

Willow then took a deep, steadying breath and

gave the teacher an encouraging look. 'I'm Willow . . . Willow Moss? There's no reason to be scared . . .'

She looked from him to a little girl who had started crying and back again. The crying got louder. The teacher's eyes continued to bulge.

'Erm. Blink if you can hear me,' she said.

The teacher, dutifully, blinked.

Willow tried to explain. 'Um . . . my mother wrote a note?' She held it up like a white flag declaring a ceasefire.

The teacher seemed to recover slightly, finally unsticking himself from the wall to take the folded-up piece of paper from her.

'I'll just sit down over here, all right?' suggested Willow, heading to a vacant desk near the centre of the classroom. She was surprised and pleased when Peg came to sit next to her.

'Y-yes,' squeaked the teacher as he began to read the letter, the blood draining further from his face.

Dear Sir,

We are proud to be sending our youngest child, Willow Moss, to attend your school. What a time to be alive! We – her parents – are delighted at the amendment to the treaty. I can only imagine your own excitement – I just wish I was there to witness it!

I can't foresee a teacher of your fine calibre having any doubts about managing someone with a magical ability. (I'm sure there will have been rigorous training for this new endeavour, and I trust that only the most stalwart of educators have made the grade.) However, if you experience even a momentary twinge of concern, have no fear! I can reassure you that in sending you Willow, who is the least dangerous of my three witch daughters, there will be no risk of her blowing up any of your students or sending them hurtling through the sky with her mind! (Kids, am I right?)

Admittedly, there is the small but, alas, real danger that she might make one or all of the children disappear due to an ability she acquired in recent months. (We blame puberty – it's havoc.) Nonetheless, rest assured in the knowledge that, for the most part, she has this under control (except when she sneezes) and is able to return those she has vanished fairly unscathed. No doubt this will offer complete comfort all round.

In terms of her educational background, Willow has been home-schooled by her granny – the renowned potion-maker Florence Moss – who has sadly passed on. However, as my mother-in-law had lost most of her marbles before she died, due to a potion explosion in the mountains of Nach, this means you may have your work cut out for you. Sorry.

Sincerely,

Raine Moss

Resident witch of neighbouring Grinfog, renowned seer and creator of the Travelling Fortune Fair*

*Tickets available by raven, half-price for the Midnight Market (sale offer for the period of the Greening Moon only)

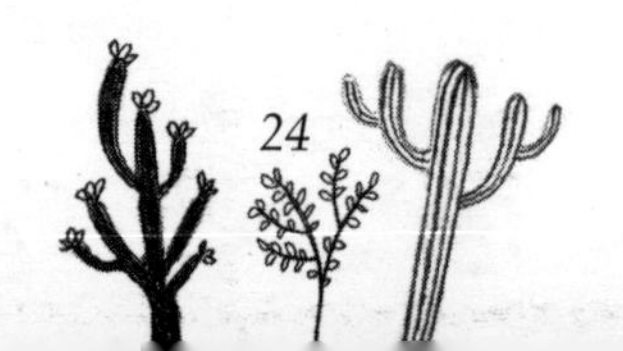

The teacher blinked a few times as he read, then reread, the letter – perhaps in the hope that it was all some sort of dream. Finally, he looked at Willow the way someone might contemplate a large spider.

'Do you . . . um, feel well?'

'Perfectly, thank you.'

He cleared his throat, then glanced at the letter again, his skin mottling slightly. 'No . . . er . . . c-colds or s-sniffles at all?'

It took a moment for Willow to grasp what he was referring to. 'Oh, that? I feel fine! Besides, I recently worked out that if I hold my nose when I sneeze, no one seems to disappear.'

Another shockwave went through the class.

The truth was that when she had done that – held her sneeze in – she had made *herself* vanish instead. Only for a minute. But Willow filed this information under 'Things Best Left Unsaid'.

'And the, um . . . creature? We don't usually allow . . . pets.'

'A WOT?' came Oswin's outraged voice from the carpetbag, which began, worryingly, to smoke.

Willow pulled a grim face and shot back quickly, 'That's all right, as Oswin isn't a pet. And he won't cause a problem.' She turned to Oswin's now pumpkin-orange eye, just visible through a hole in the hairy bag, with an expression that threatened . . . consequences. The sort of consequences that resulted in a *bath*.

There was a sulky sort of grunt from inside. **'Fine. But 'tis bad enough when these cumberworlds fink I is a cat. "Pet" jes takes the blimmerings cake. No respect, an' me being the last kobold an' all . . .'**

'Um, right. V-very well. Erm. Welcome, Willow. I am Master Cuttlefish,' said the teacher, patting himself down in his nervousness, as if to assure himself of who he was. He glanced at the hairy green bag at Willow's feet, then chose to simply ignore it, which was probably wise.

Willow felt someone tugging on her sleeve and turned to find Peg looking at her with wide green eyes. Up close, she noticed that he had a smattering of freckles across his nose. 'You can make people vanish?'

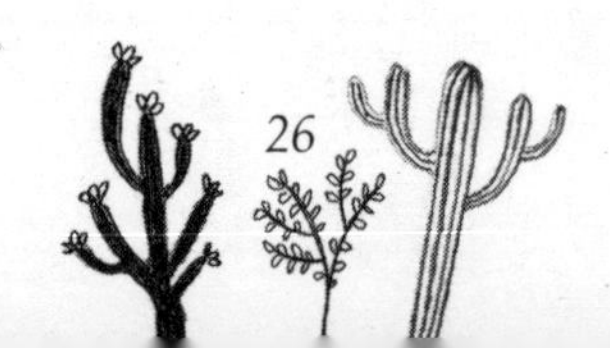

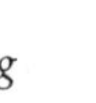

The spirit hare stood in the clearing.

'You have what I have asked of you?' said Silas.

The hare stared at him for a long moment, then opened its mouth. It made a hacking, coughing sound, then something round and grey rolled towards him.

It was an eye.

A clouded eye.

Silas bent down and picked it up gingerly. The thing looked dead, but as he touched the eye it grew darker, like a day shrouded in fog.

The wind began to whistle, and up ahead a storm gathered.

Silas allowed himself the smallest glimmer of a smile. 'You have done well.'

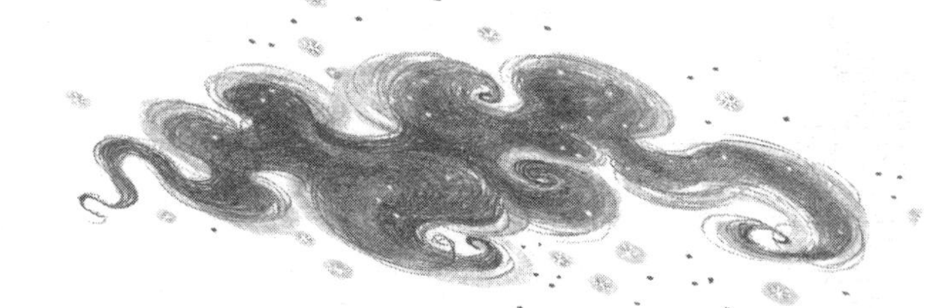

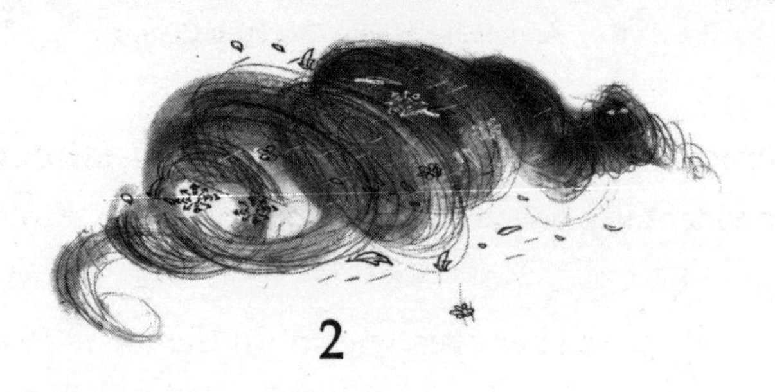

2

Something Windy This Way Comes

Willow gave an embarrassed sort of nod in response to Peg's question. 'You know I find lost things, right?' She had helped Peg find a few things in the past – he seemed to have a habit of misplacing his fishing flies as she recalled.

He nodded.

'But making them vanish started happening last year,' she continued. 'Do you remember . . . Elth Night?'

Peg stared, then after a moment he clapped a hand over his mouth and sniggered. 'So it WAS you! *You* were the reason Birdy Pondwater found herself starkers at the bunfire.'

Willow blushed crimson.

Technically, the old woman still had on a pair of red-and-white striped bloomers, so she wasn't

exactly stark-naked, but yes: Willow had somehow, accidentally, made the old woman's dress vanish . . . in public.

She closed her eyes, wincing at the memory. It was not one of her finest moments. When she opened them, Peg was still staring at her, looking amused.

'I believed you when you said it wasn't you . . . You know, before the villagers threw their currant buns at you, and your sister dragged you off.' He grinned, revealing a dimple in his cheek.

Willow fought back a grin herself. 'Juniper didn't drag me off. She . . . er . . . marched me firmly away from the stampeding horde.'

'Oh right . . . That's totally different.'

'Yep.'

They shared a grin.

'Erm, but it turns out it *was* me . . . though I didn't know that at the time. My magic started to go a bit haywire – or at least that's what I thought was happening. It's a long story, but I've developed the other side of my ability. Now, as well as finding things, I can make them disappear. People too . . . though mostly by accident. I can't quite get it right on purpose.'

She didn't tell Peg that, when she tried, she usually made the wrong person vanish – like her mum when she was really aiming for her sister Camille. It had caused more than a few awkward moments at home and plenty of time spent in the attic, where she was supposed to 'think about her behaviour' while Camille gloated at her from the stairs . . . and so the cycle repeated itself.

It was quite a relief that her sisters were too old for the new mixed schools.

To Willow's surprise, instead of looking scared at the prospect of vanishing, Peg's face split into a mischievous smile. 'It's a pity you haven't got it nailed down just yet,' he said, casting the teacher a sideways glance. 'That could come in handy. You have no idea how boring Cuttlefish can get when he puts his mind to it. And he *always* puts his mind to it.'

Willow chuckled softly.

Peg's face turned serious for a moment and he whispered, 'It's wild that you're here, though. My mum couldn't believe it when she heard that they'd changed the rules . . .' His smile faltered, and he looked a bit sheepish. 'She's a bit, er . . . old-fashioned.'

Willow nodded. She'd guessed as much. His mother, Begonia, always wore a 'witch-resistant necklace'. It

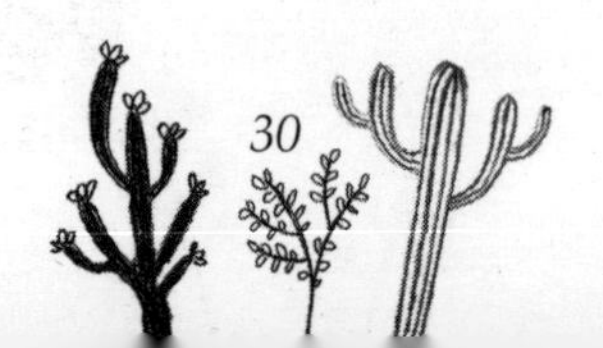

was made out of goat hair and wigweed sprouts and was supposedly meant to protect the wearer against magic. It didn't work, but Willow would never tell Peg that.

When she was little, Willow had passed Begonia in the street, and something about the way the woman had clutched at her necklace had struck Willow as odd. She'd gone to find Granny Flossy – who had been brewing up a potion for improved digestion that would later destroy part of the greenhouse – to tell her about what had happened.

Granny had moved aside a long strand of green hair and looked up at Willow in surprise. 'That necklace Begonia wears? It's jes old bits and bobs strung together – they sell them at some of the markets. I've even made a few of them meself in me time, ter smooth things over when us magical folk started

moving inter their towns. It won' do much apart from keep the fleas off her. Best not ter let on, though,' she'd said, tapping the side of her nose. 'Sometimes ye've got ter let people have something ter believe in so their fears don' take 'em over.'

Willow had been a bit shocked. 'You've made them yourself – even though you know they don't work? Isn't that, well, a bit . . . wrong?'

Granny Flossy had considered the question while cutting up a bunch of grumbling Gertrudes for her potion – probably to disguise the bad taste. The purple juice stained her fingers. 'Fear is a dark mistress, and it don' play fair, child. It'll take up all the room in yer brain if yer let it, so it's a kindness ter find ways ter help people keep it at bay. 'Tisn't exactly right or wrong, but a bit of both – like life itself, which is a mix too. You see?'

And Willow had. But she knew that not everyone would.

She looked at Peg, who seemed a bit embarrassed. 'I wish she wouldn't wear that necklace,' he said softly. 'I mean, she knows there's nothing to fear really . . .'

'It's fine, Peg. I don't mind.'

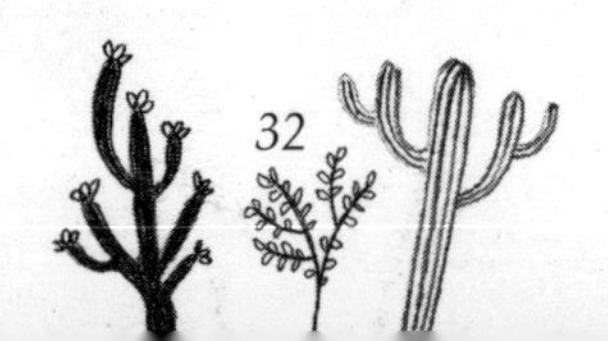

Part of Willow wished she had a load of those necklaces now, so that she could offer them to the rest of the class and make them feel better. But a bigger part of her wished that they wouldn't want them, that the children would see for themselves that they didn't have to be afraid just because she was a bit different.

Peg sighed. 'I mean, it's silly that Mum's still a bit wary of witches. All I've seen your family do is help people, and she knows that too, I think . . . She even said that you have a right to learn just as much as any of us. But, considering how scared people are, it's a bit weird that they changed things, um, so suddenly, from one week to the next.' He looked embarrassed. 'Um, not that they shouldn't have.'

Willow was quick to reassure him. 'No, you're right. It *is* weird . . .'

She thought once again of how little her own parents had listened to her concerns, and how much it had convinced her that something wasn't right . . .

A few weeks ago, her parents had attended an Enchancil meeting informing them of the new legislation. When they'd come home and told Willow the 'happy news', it was like waking up in a house that you thought you

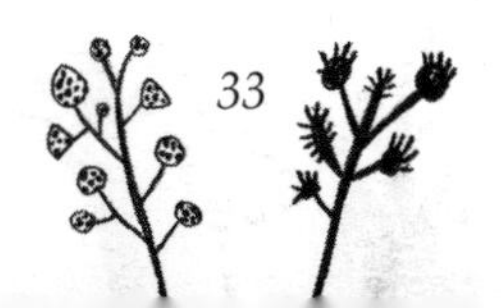

knew, only to find yourself tumbling down a set of stairs you never realised existed.

They'd looked blissfully happy about the idea of sending their youngest daughter to a school governed by the Brothers of Wol – an order now headed by the person Willow and her friends had discovered was actively trying to steal everyone's magic and start another war.

'You can't be serious?' Willow had cried. 'Why on Starfell would you choose to trust Silas, after everything that's happened?'

Willow's mother, Raine, had tutted. 'The Enchancil have cleared all that up. It was just a silly misunderstanding . . .'

'A . . . *misunderstanding*?' Willow had stared at them both in shock. Just two weeks before, when Silas had been appointed, her mother had said they needed to find Moreg and that it was time to take a stand against the Brothers . . . and now this? Suddenly she thought it was all right to send her youngest child to a school run by these people?

'Oh yes, my dear, it's nothing for us to worry about,' her father had said.

Willow had blinked, looking from one parent to the other. From underneath the table, there had been

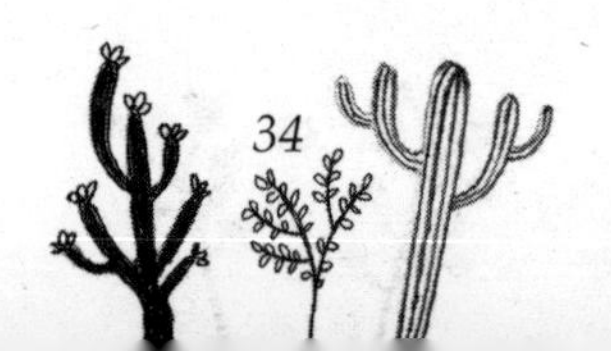

a faint **'Wot?'** from Oswin, who seemed as confused as she was.

Willow stared. 'But . . . we *know* what Silas wants, and he's getting even stronger – he's overthrown the Brothers of Wol. Can't you see how suspicious it is that he's now inviting magical children into his schools?'

Raine had huffed. 'Overthrown? Don't be silly. He's been voted in as leader. That's how it works. And, as for "suspicious", you just sound paranoid. Things change. This is what real progress looks like! You simply got the wrong information, that's all . . .'

Willow had continued to stare at her parents in disbelief. 'The wrong information? When my friend *saw* Silas's own memories, proving that he's trying to become the most powerful magician in our history? That he's planning to rip all the magic out of Starfell?'

'Yes, that's just nonsense. It's why we need to send you all to school, you see, so you can sharpen your minds, accept the truth.'

Willow had spluttered, 'Accept the truth? The only truth that needs accepting is that Silas *must be stopped*!'

Why were her parents acting like this?

Willow's father had shaken his head benignly. 'Oh, Fetch,' he'd said, using an unfortunate nickname that

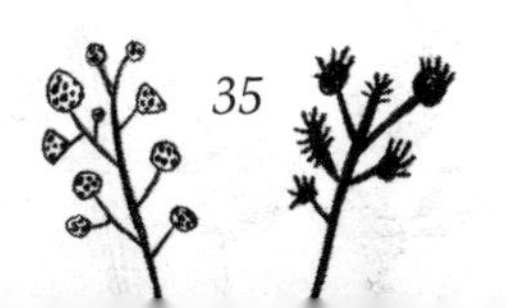

Camille had started when she was little and Willow still couldn't quite shake off. 'It's all going to be just wonderful, you'll see.'

In the weeks that followed, Willow had tried her best to get through to her parents, but they'd only looked at her with slightly vacant expressions whenever she brought up Silas or his plans. Willow had been forced to conclude that something odd had happened at that Enchancil meeting . . .

She turned to Peg. 'I was starting to worry that I was the only one who thought it was weird that the Brothers suddenly wanted us in their schools!'

It was good to have someone agree with her. It hadn't occurred to Willow that it must have seemed very odd from the non-magical community's perspective too.

'Nope,' he said, then jerked his head in the direction of a few of the other children who were still cowering beneath their desks. 'I bet they think it's odd too . . . if I were to take a wild guess.'

Willow gave a hollow laugh.

'But maybe it's nice that it's happening,' he said.

Willow looked from Peg to the other children, who

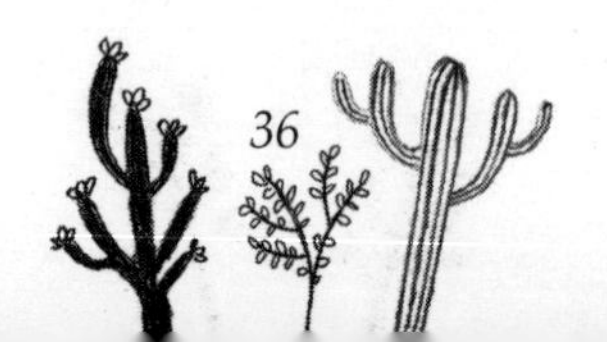

had now picked up their chairs and desks to get as far away from her as possible. Somehow, she thought, despite Peg's kindness, 'nice' was a stretch. In fact, she was a bit worried that the Brothers were trying too hard to make things seem 'nice'.

Master Cuttlefish called for their attention as he picked up a box from the floor.

'Instructions and workbooks from the Brothers of Wol, for our n-new undertaking,' he said. 'We were instructed to only open this box if one of you actually showed up.' He broke off, cleared his throat and took out the instructions. As he read, he picked up several pieces of chalk from within the box and muttered, 'Ah! That is a relief. I wondered if the Brothers had completely lost their minds . . . Though, of course, I shouldn't have doubted their wisdom . . . Oh yes, indeed. I see now.'

From near Willow's feet, there came a faint **'Wot's 'e on about?'**

'I don't know,' whispered Willow, feeling the hairs begin to prickle on the back of her neck. She shared a confused look with the kobold, whose green eye was just visible through a small hole in the carpetbag.

The teacher straightened and it was as if all his

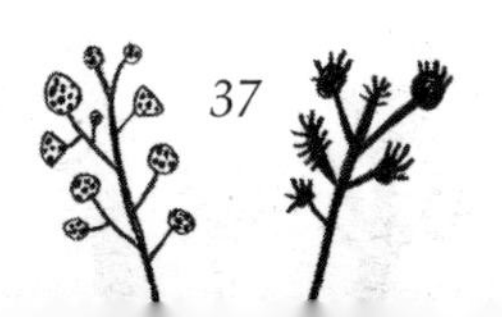

earlier fear had left him. The colour returned to his cheeks and he called out, 'Nigel?'

The ginger-haired boy at the back who had made the sign of Wol at Willow squeaked in reply, 'Yes, master?'

'Please come over here and help distribute these.'

Nigel hesitated for a moment, as it meant passing Willow, but then went to help Cuttlefish hand out the thin blue volumes to the class.

When one of them landed on Willow's desk, she stared at it. In the middle was a large 'W' embossed on the cover in red.

But, before she could open the book, the sky outside suddenly turned the colour of an old bruise. The air crackled with electricity and the classroom door was flung open, slamming against the wall with an enormous crash.

'Oh nooooo,' cried Oswin. **'Oh no, oh, me greedy aunt! Wot new eel is this?'**

Willow blanched. What new 'eel' indeed?

The air had turned cold and the wind began to howl as something wild, something blue, something utterly *terrifying* came hurtling towards them.

It was a tornado.

Everyone began to scream blue murder. Wind

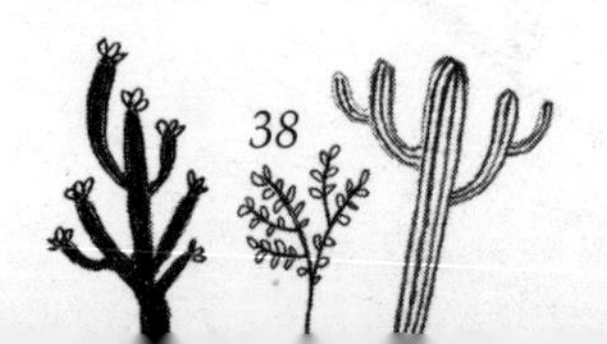

whipped through the classroom at a rate of knots, overturning desks, blowing papers everywhere and frosting everything with ice.

The hairy green bag began to shake as Oswin zipped himself more securely inside. **'I really should 'ave stayed under the bed today,'** he whimpered.

There was an eerie wailing sound, loud enough to break glass, and, as the swirling mass came closer, everyone gasped in shock.

Right in the centre of the whirlwind was a girl.

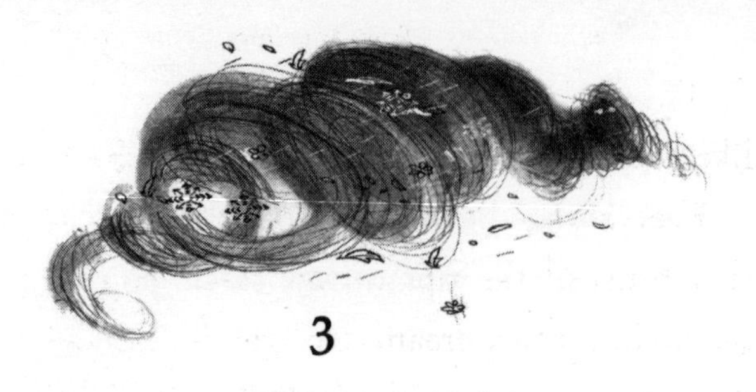

3

Twist Howling

Frost spread across the floor as the girl spun into the classroom.

Willow shivered violently in her thin green cloak, her eyelashes crusting with icicles.

And then, quite as suddenly as it had appeared, the wind and the cold and the swirling blue tornado died down, revealing a tall girl around Willow's age. Her hair was white and appeared to crackle as it quivered around her head in a kind of electrified cloud. She inspected the class with piercing blue eyes – the kind that seemed not only to see you but take an X-ray too. Then she calmly told the icy wind, which was now swirling more gently by her side, '*Selia – scatter now.*'

And it did, departing in an intricate swirl of mist and ice.

When the girl saw the many pairs of fearful eyes,

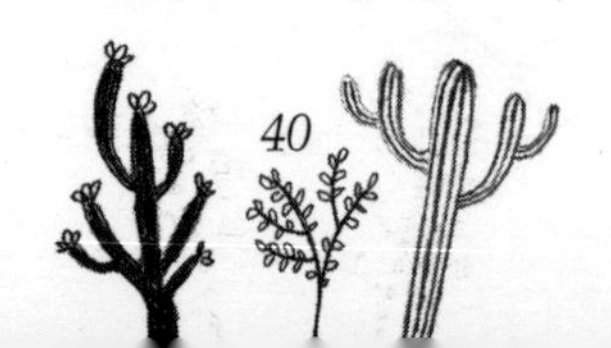

like peeled grapefruits, pinned on her, she frowned.

Everything she wore – from the long white dress that brushed the tips of her black, pointed, lace-up boots, to a thick cream cardigan – was twisted. Yet, despite the fact that she looked a bit like she'd been dragged backwards through a hedge, met the resident wildlife, got into a fight and *won* . . . she was somehow still elegant. Willow was reminded of the way an old house can sometimes seem both stately and slightly dilapidated at the same time.

The girl's pale eyes took in the fallen desks and she sighed. 'Skiron can be a real menace indoors. North winds, you know?' she said.

None of them did know. They all blinked at her in horror.

Unfortunately, the fierce, swirling, frosty wind that was lurking just outside the classroom door seemed to take sudden offence at the girl's words. A screeching, ear-splitting noise erupted, making all the children clap their hands over their ears, as the wind gusted itself into a furious frenzy and hurtled inside once more.

The girl tapped her foot impatiently, lips pursed. 'Skiron, it's not like you to be so sensitive. Honestly, you're embarrassing yourself.'

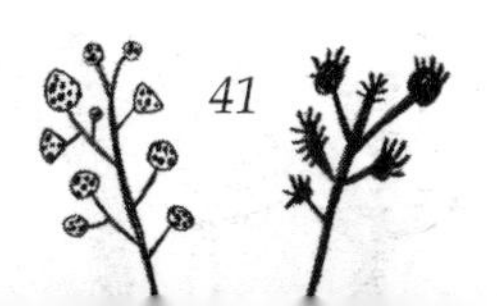

This, unfortunately, made things worse.

The door began to slam violently on its hinges, and the wind swelled to three times its size as it spun like a top into the centre of the room. Everyone screamed as desks and chairs and children started to rise into the air.

Clouds of condensation left their mouths and ice crystals hardened on the floor. Inside the hairy green bag, Willow could hear Oswin's teeth chattering, along with a muffled **'Oh nooo, oh, me 'orrid aunt . . . Oh, fings is turning blue which should not be blue . . .'**

Some of the children managed to hold on tight to their desks or chairs, their legs floating behind them, but others were thrown roughly against the walls, their screams reaching a deafening pitch.

Willow winced as Nigel, the ginger-haired boy, was gusted upwards, and there was a nasty cracking sound when his head met the ceiling.

This made Willow's entrance seem like a breeze in comparison. She gingerly got out of her chair, fighting hard against the fierce wind, and edged towards the girl. Willow's lips were turning blue from the freezing cold, and she wasn't sure what she was going to *do* exactly, but she hoped to help.

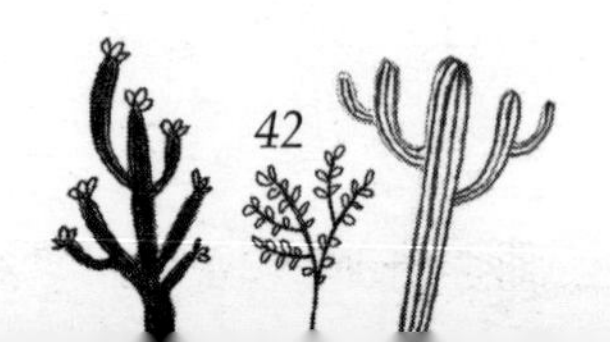

However, it soon became clear that help was not needed.

The girl used that strange word again: '*Selia.*' But nothing happened. She raised an eyebrow, then said in a low voice that was only mildly terrifying, 'I am going to count to three, but it would be better for us both if you decide to be reasonable and obey the command before that happens.'

The wind was being – there was no other word for it – stubborn. At that moment, in sulky response, it knocked over a big wall display that featured the children's artwork.

The girl's eyes glittered. Thunder rumbled as if from nowhere, and it took a moment for Willow to note that it had come from the girl's open mouth as she boomed, 'ONE!'

Everyone flinched.

'Oh noooo! Don' make her count ter free!' cried Oswin, the top of his head peeking out of the bag. **'Oh, me heart!'**

The wind, it seemed, agreed. It beat a hasty retreat through the classroom door.

With that, the temperature returned to normal. The frost melted away as suddenly as it had appeared.

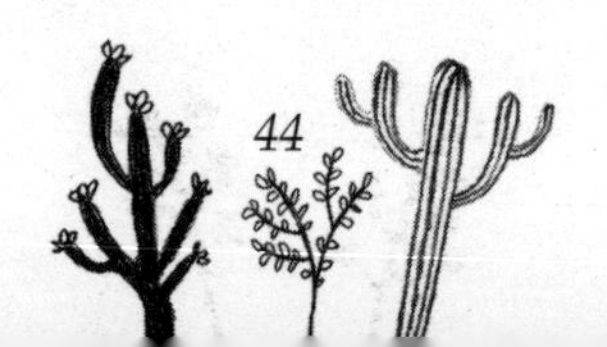

The classroom furniture and a handful of children came tumbling to the floor with a crash.

The windswept girl, however, made no comment. Perhaps she was used to this. Instead, she turned back to the class as if it were completely normal to have thunder coming out of your mouth. 'Sometimes you have to bring the thunder to avoid the lightning,' she explained. Then she smiled, which was also a bit terrifying.

'To tell you the truth,' she added, rubbing her throat, 'it doesn't half burn when it comes out. My Aunt Dot says gargling with salt water helps strengthen the vocal cords, but so far nothing . . . Then again,' she snorted, 'she's got the west wind – the gentlest one, which brings along spring, you know? It's not like she ever needs to call on the thunder when her wind, Zephyrus, ignores the command to scatter. She can just summon a slight drizzle and hers just flies away, absolutely terrified. Skiron, on the other hand, is one of the toughest and the fiercest – that's why he's mine,' she smirked.

Willow's mouth had been hanging open, and that's when the girl finally noticed her. She seemed a little amused or surprised – it was hard to tell. 'Were you coming to help?'

'Um, y-yes.'

The girl stared. 'Can you tame winds too?'

'Er, no . . .' admitted Willow. 'Not at all. That was, well, brilliant, what you did. I just thought maybe you could use a hand?' Then she blushed. 'Um, but obviously you had it under control.'

The girl's pale eyes regarded her for some time. 'Yes, I certainly did,' she said, then she frowned. 'But you didn't know that. You came to help, despite having no ability to do so . . . which tells me something. You're either a bit odd, or you're a witch.' Her eyes danced. 'Probably a bit of both.'

Willow didn't know whether to feel insulted or not, but she could tell that, if anything, the girl seemed to warm to her. Besides, if Willow were honest with herself, she'd lost the battle with being 'a bit odd' a long time ago.

She decided it was best to change the subject. 'I can't believe another witch has lived near me this whole time!'

The girl looked askance. 'A witch? I should think not.'

Willow blinked in surprise. 'B-but—'

'I'm an elf.'

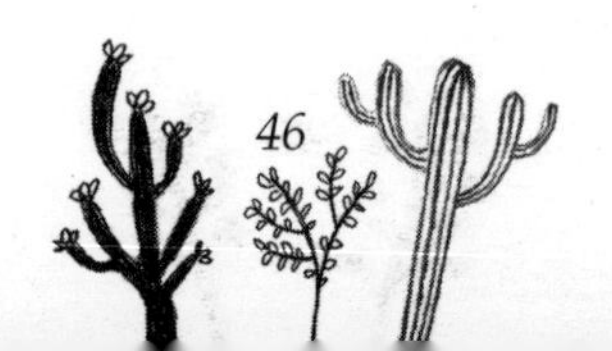

Willow's eyes shone in amazement as she noticed the girl's pointed ears. 'Oh!'

Elves kept themselves to themselves, so she'd never actually met one before. She knew they were excellent craftspeople and traders of magic, though, and some of the best magical objects and devices – like Moreg's portal cloak – came from the elvish city of Lael. The girl's storm magic also made a little more sense now, as it was only elves who seemed to have some control over the weather. (Well, elves and Moreg Vaine, who could make lightning and thunder strike too – though, to be fair, *not out of her mouth.*) And, unlike humans, who didn't always get any magical ability, all elves did, though no one really knew why.

Elves were also rumoured to have some kind of collective magical power called elfsense. Willow wasn't sure how it worked, but then not many humans did.

'I'm Twist Howling,' said the girl, holding up her index finger. Seeing that Willow clearly didn't know what she was meant to do, Twist's mouth curved into a small smile, and she picked up Willow's hand to touch her finger to Willow's own. A small blueish-green

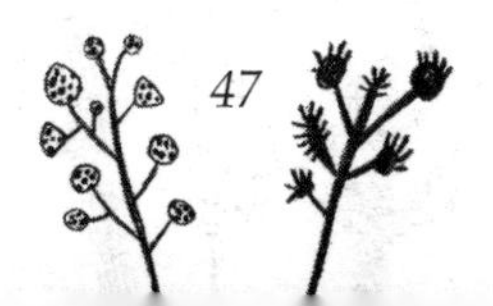

spark emitted from them both, which took Willow by surprise.

'Knew you were a witch,' the elf girl said.

'I'm Willow Moss,' said Willow, still a bit puzzled by the sparks.

The girl's eyes widened in surprise. 'YOU'RE Willow Moss?' She didn't let Willow's hand go. In fact, she pulled her closer to get a better look.

The way Twist was staring made Willow feel a little awkward. There were some people in the magical community who had heard of her now, mostly due to the reporting in the *Grimoire Gazette* – which, unfortunately, made her sound like she needed to be carted off somewhere.

'Er, yes. I've, um, been mentioned in the Enchancil newsletter . . . a few times.'

Twist let out an odd barking laugh that made a few of the children jump in their seats. 'A few times? It's been every week without fail for the past three months.' Then she frowned. 'They don't seem to like you much.'

Willow didn't know what to say. It wasn't untrue.

'Well,' Twist carried on, 'you're the reason I came to this school. I wanted to track you down. I need to talk to you.'

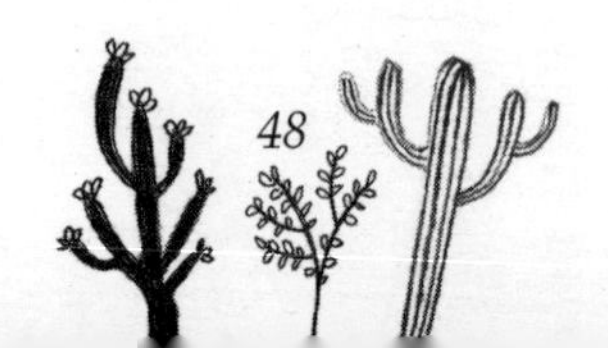

Willow's eyes bulged and she took an involuntary step backwards.

From the hairy carpetbag, there came a whispered '***Oh no.***'

Which was probably what Willow's knees would say too, if they could speak.

The fiercest person she'd met since *Moreg Vaine* had come to track her down?

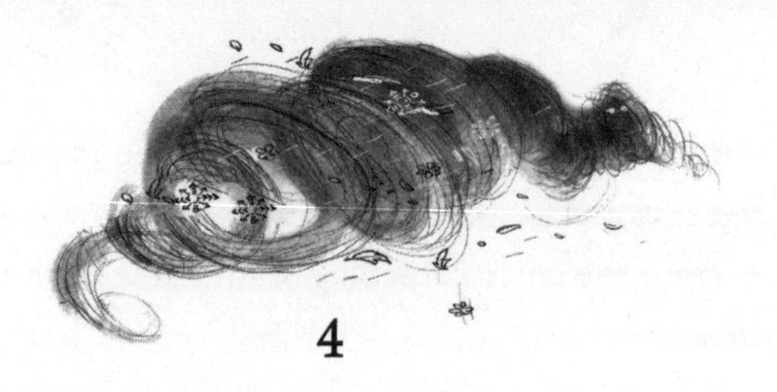

4

An Elvish Legend

'Really?' said Willow, finally managing to pull her fingers from Twist's grasp. 'Um, w-why did you want to talk to me?'

But Willow wasn't to learn why just yet, as right then there was the sound of a throat being cleared rather loudly.

It was Master Cuttlefish. He had managed not to stick himself to the wall at Twist's arrival, and it appeared that his impatience at her continued interruption of his lesson had, at last, outweighed his fear.

'If you two have quite finished getting acquainted? Not to mention destroying my classroom before we've even started our first lesson?' he added sarcastically.

Willow blushed. 'Sorry,' she said.

Twist, however, did not apologise. She merely

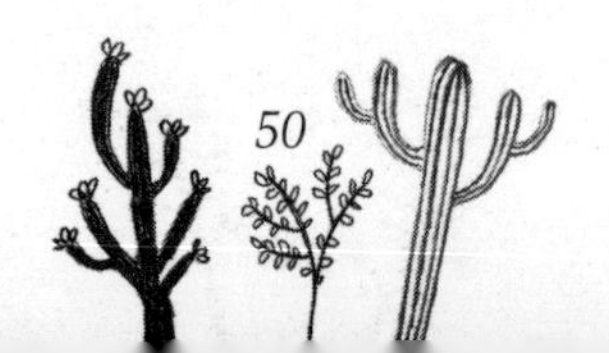

stared at Cuttlefish until he cleared his throat again and said, a bit more politely, 'I-I presume you're also starting with us today?' His tone implied that he wasn't exactly thrilled about this.

And, to be fair, given the state of his classroom – which now looked rather worse for wear, the children windswept and dishevelled with tracks of tears down their faces, skin mottled from screaming – he might have had good reason to feel put out.

Twist nodded. 'Yes. I had a note, but there's a strong possibility it got blown away . . .'

'You don't say,' he muttered. 'Well, never mind. I think I get the gist: new student, magic, lucky me.'

Willow shared a look of surprise with Oswin, who muttered, **'Someone 'as 'ad a change o' heart.'**

Willow agreed. Cuttlefish had indeed made a remarkable recovery in his approach to magical children in a relatively short space of time, considering his earlier fear of her.

'Class started twenty minutes ago, Miss Twist. Do not be late again,' he said.

Twist didn't reply. She simply cocked her head to one side and stared at him with those odd, piercing eyes of hers.

After a rather awkward moment, as Cuttlefish grew ever paler, he suggested weakly, 'Er, p-please. T-take a seat.'

The rest of the class gave them both a wide berth, setting their now-righted desks and chairs down as far away as possible. The two girls were left in the centre, like a small leper colony. Only Peg stayed near, giving them both a shaky smile. He touched his throat for a moment and Willow wondered if he was thinking about borrowing his mother's necklace after all . . .

Cuttlefish handed Twist one of the blue books. Then he turned, walked over to the classroom door, and drew a small *x* on it with chalk. Once done, he addressed the rest of the class as if this were perfectly normal behaviour.

'Welcome back, everyone. Before we get started on the new curriculum, I think a brief recap of what we learnt last year might be helpful for our old and, er, new students,' he said, and his voice took on a monotonous drone as he began going over what they had covered the year before, most of which seemed to involve methods of farming.

Within minutes, Willow was finding it hard to pay attention . . . and she wondered if the Brothers of

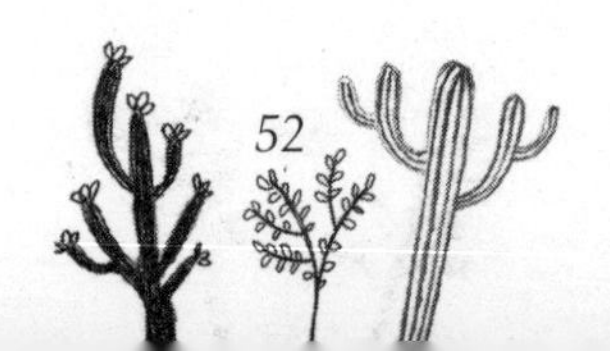

Wol's plan was simply to bore magical children into submission.

'Told you,' whispered Peg. 'He takes being boring seriously.'

Willow grinned, then introduced Peg to Twist.

Twist nodded at him in greeting, then tilted her head at the chalk on the door, whispering, 'What's with that? Is it something to do with the lesson?'

Peg shook his head. 'No idea! First time he's ever done that.'

There was a harrumph from the hairy carpetbag and Twist turned to it in confusion. 'That's Oswin,' Willow said quietly. 'He's a kobold. I'll explain later.'

From within the bag, Oswin muttered, **'Can yew smells that? That chalk smells a bit weirds.'**

'What?' asked Willow, but she was distracted when Cuttlefish asked the old students to take out their notebooks and summarise some of last year's lessons. A boy at the back of the classroom was asked to outline the history of farming in Grinfog, and he started on a long monologue about the types of apples they grew in their county. A girl with pigtails was next, describing the different harvesting methods and how they had changed over the years.

Willow found herself stifling several yawns.

'Oh no,' whispered Oswin. **'I'm actually gonna be bored ter death. The Flossy Mistress always made learnin' much better than this – excitings . . . cos yew never knew if she wos gonna blow the roofs off again or not.'**

Willow felt tears smart in her eyes.

'I miss that,' Oswin said mournfully.

Willow had to bite her lip to stop it from wobbling. 'Me too,' she whispered.

Granny Flossy's lessons had been about life and, despite what her mother thought, Willow knew her grandmother's wisdom was probably a lot more valuable than knowing the various types of apple rot, which Peg was now reluctantly reciting.

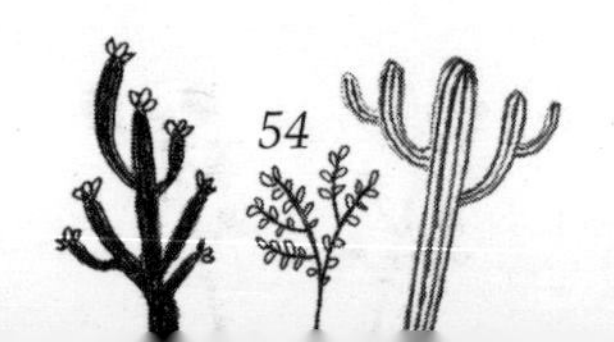

Before Willow could get swept away in her memories, though, she was interrupted by Twist.

'Willow, like I said – I need to talk to you. This week's *Gazette* – did you read it?'

Willow nodded. 'Look, I know everyone thinks I'm sick or mad or making things up to get attention, but that's not true. It's Silas – he can't be trusted.'

Twist stared at her as if she were an idiot. 'Course he can't. We all know that.'

Willow blinked in confusion.

Twist went on, 'By "we", I mean elves. I don't know why all the other magical folk have suddenly decided to accept everything Silas and the Brothers are saying . . . I mean, it doesn't make sense, does it?'

'Exactly!' cried Willow in an agitated whisper. 'That's what I've been thinking. It's like something happened at the last Enchancil meeting – since then, it's as if all the grown-ups have just decided to blindly trust Silas and the Brothers, ignoring everything else. I mean, until then my parents had been quite suspicious of them.'

'Interesting . . . We elves haven't had a seat on the Enchancil for years. We were thrown off after a bit of an incident. My Aunt Tuppence lost her temper when she caught someone lying . . . She *may* have overreacted a little, blasting him with a bolt of lightning – you know, the usual stuff – but maybe that explains why the elves feel differently . . . because they weren't there?'

'That would make sense!' said Willow, though a small, dismayed part of her was picturing Twist's aunt blasting someone with a lightning bolt . . . But she managed to push that thought aside for the moment. 'My parents have been impossible to reason with ever since that meeting. That's why I came here today – to see for myself what the Brothers are really planning with this new idea to mix magical and non-magical children together. Something about it just feels . . . weird. I don't know what they're up to, but I want to find out.'

Twist smiled. 'Well, I figured you'd be trying to do just that. I was sure I'd find you here.'

Willow stared at her in surprise. 'So . . . what *did* you want to talk to me about?'

'It's about Silas. I think he stole the scroll.'

'What scroll?'

Twist looked impatient. 'The ancient elvish scroll

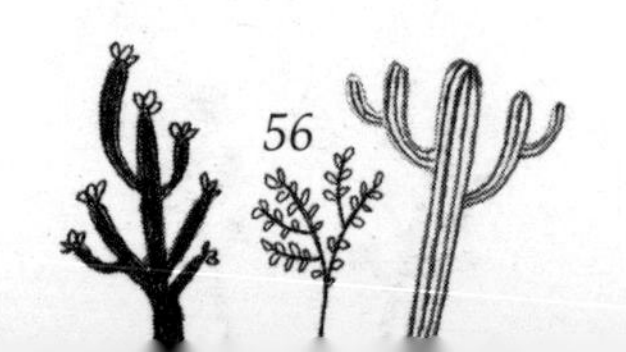

that was stolen from Library!'

Willow frowned. She vaguely remembered there had been a string of burglaries throughout Starfell lately, including the theft of an old scroll, but she hadn't paid much attention, to be honest. She had other worries to focus on – like the fact that all the grown-ups seemed to have lost the power of rational thought, for one.

'Why do you think Silas has taken it?' Willow asked carefully. Then she frowned, recalling what the *Gazette* article had said. 'No one has ever been able to decipher that scroll, right? They said it could be something as simple as an old elvish recipe for bread or whatever.' Willow remembered that part because it had been a quote from Copernica Darling, a librarian and Secret Keeper she'd met once when she visited the town of Library.

To her surprise, Twist let out a short laugh. 'They're lying! That's their job as Secret Keepers. *Of course* they know what the scroll says!'

Willow blinked.

'Okay, well, not in detail,' Twist continued. 'I don't think they've lied about not being able to translate it properly. But all elves know that it contains the last

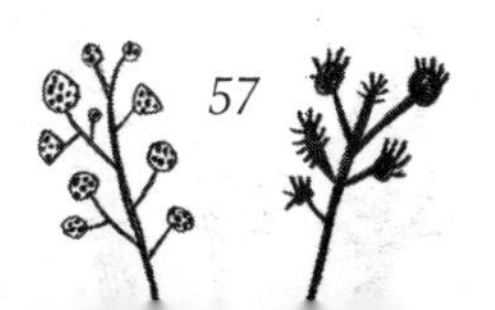

words of Queen Almefeira and the truth about what happened to the vanished elvish kingdom . . .'

Willow had heard the stories over the years about the kingdom of Llandunia that had mysteriously disappeared during the Long War, and the infamous scroll that had appeared afterwards with the queen's seal. She'd always thought it was just a story really – a fairy tale about a beautiful queen and a land that had gone missing a thousand years ago.

'But isn't that just a myth?'

Twist gave her a hard stare. 'No,' she said firmly. 'Though humans love to dismiss my people's history as mere fairy tale.'

Willow stared at the elf as she took that in. 'So you think Silas knows this, and wants to try to find the kingdom? Why?'

Twist darted a look over her shoulder. A boy at the back of the class was still going over crop-rotation methods. Twist's white-blonde hair seemed to crackle as she leant nearer to Willow and whispered, 'Because there's a part of the story that no one knows, and it's linked to Queen Almefeira's staff.'

'Her staff?' echoed Willow.

Twist nodded. 'It was said to have enormous power –

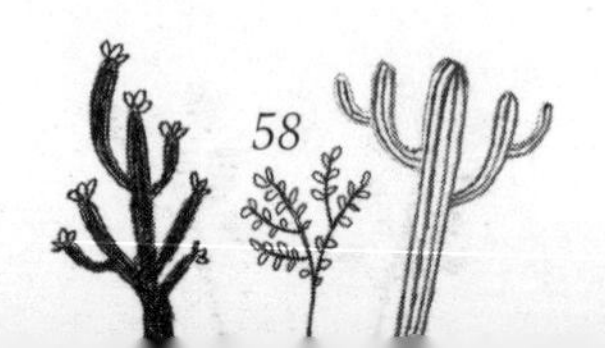

even the ability to bestow the gift of magic. Now, when the kingdom vanished, so did the queen, and so did her staff. Most people know this.' She leant closer still. 'But the part they don't know is something I just found out. It's the reason I came to find you, Willow. There was another side to her staff, a darker one: *it could take magic away.*'

Willow gasped, the colour draining from her face. 'How do you know?'

'I found something, back in Lael. It will be easier to show you. But I think you're right. Silas *is* going to try to steal everyone's magic – he just needs to find the staff first.'

Willow paled. 'This is how he plans on doing it.'

Twist nodded. 'And what's worse is I think he's probably quite close to finding it. Think about it: that's why he was so keen to suddenly allow us into his schools. He's about to get his hands on a staff that can strip away magic – so he's started to round up the first people he can use it on.'

Willow blinked in horror as it all became horribly clear.

Twist meant them.

Magical children *like them.*

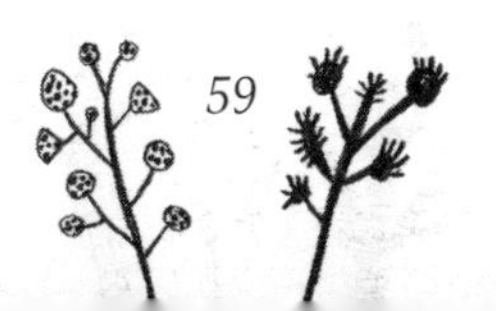

'High Master?' said the young acolyte, approaching the raised stone dais hesitantly.

Flames suddenly ignited from the torches on either side of the marble seat in which Silas sat, his fingers steepled.

'You may have an audience,' replied Silas.

It was the official welcome, and the young acolyte should have felt relieved, but instead he glanced at the flames and swallowed.

There had been rumours circling the Brotherhood before Silas became the new High Master. Whispers behind locked doors. Whispers about his strange . . . abilities. They had been told that he was blessed, that he had been touched by Wol himself. Anointed. It seemed . . . unlikely. Why him, why now . . . after all these years?

The acolyte dared not even think it, afraid it would show on his face . . . but he couldn't help himself. So much had changed in the Brotherhood. So many new

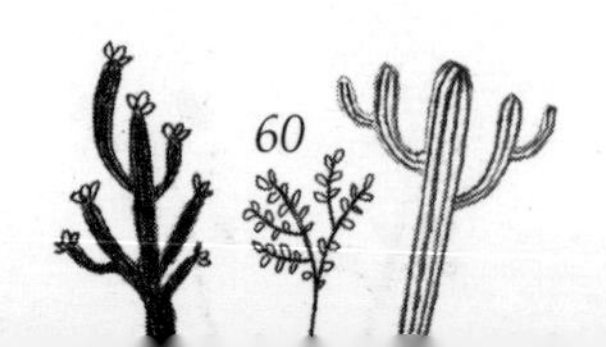

'blessings' and 'gifts' had suddenly been discovered – like the glowing manacles that could ensnare a witch. The way these tools worked seemed odd – akin almost to the devices used by an unnatural – and they all led back to Silas. There was a simpler explanation, the acolyte knew. One he wished he could stop thinking of now that it had occurred to him . . . What if Silas had simply been cursed with magic?

Over the years, there had been talk. Strange incidents that happened behind closed doors. Accidents. The old High Master had brushed them aside, refused to do anything about them.

They used to say that Silas was a foundling. Some said his mother was a witch.

But no one spoke of that any more. Not now that he was High Master. Not now that he had changed so much in such a short time. He was only a few years older than the acolyte, but one would never be able to tell that now: his face had hardened and lost all traces of the softening effects of youth. His hair, once straw-coloured and thatch-like, had been shaved, as was the custom of all High Masters. Yet he had gone a step further, not keeping the ring of hair. It was unusual, a practice that only the High Masters of old had done.

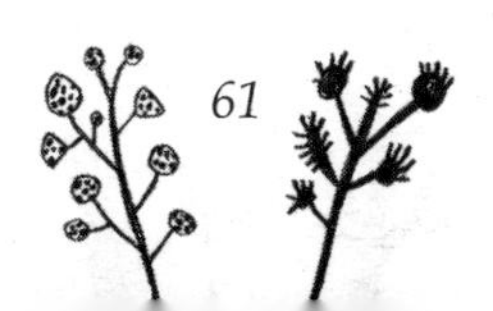

At his throat he wore a strange kind of amulet hanging from a piece of twisted brown leather. It was grey and clouded, and, as the acolyte watched, its surface seemed to shift like fog.

It was another of the strange 'blessings' that had appeared in recent months.

As if reading the acolyte's mind, Silas looked at him and said, 'You have been wondering, Elsen, about my blessing.'

Elsen stepped forward quickly, desperate to deny his misgivings, and almost tripped over his long brown robe. His mind raced. Who had he told? Just one or two Brothers, he supposed. How much would they have told Silas?

'High Master, I was only curious . . . That is all.'

'Curious about Wol's blessings? Curious enough to question a . . . god?'

Elsen's eyes widened in fear. 'No, master. Oh no – never that.' He was effusive in his denials.

To Elsen's surprise, Silas waved his hands in dismissal. 'It is natural to wonder, of course.'

Elsen breathed a sigh of relief.

'Step closer, and I will show you Wol's blessing.'

The boy hesitated. But then he walked the few

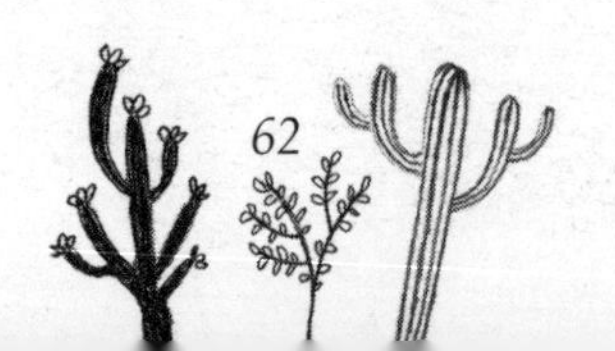

steps towards the High Master, trying and failing to avoid Silas's penetrating eyes. He noticed that he had stepped over a faint chalk line, which seemed odd; the High Master was so particular about cleanliness and presentation . . .

Before he reached the top step, there was a screeching sound and he was knocked several feet in the air and came crashing down a few feet away.

He lay on the stone floor, winded, dazed and confused.

Silas stood up, and Elsen could see that his robes were very different to the old High Master's. These were long and black, and instead of the single arrow in the centre, there was another more ancient symbol, of a spiralled stick topped with a pair of half-moons surrounding a circle.

He walked nonchalantly towards the boy and looked down at him.

The young acolyte was blinking up at him in surprise. But there was no fear in his eyes. Not any longer.

'I have been chosen, you see. Chosen by Wol to be his successor,' said Silas.

The boy's eyes appeared almost blank, but he readily agreed. 'Yes, High Master. I see now.'

'Good,' said Silas. 'You may spread the word.'

'I would be honoured to.'

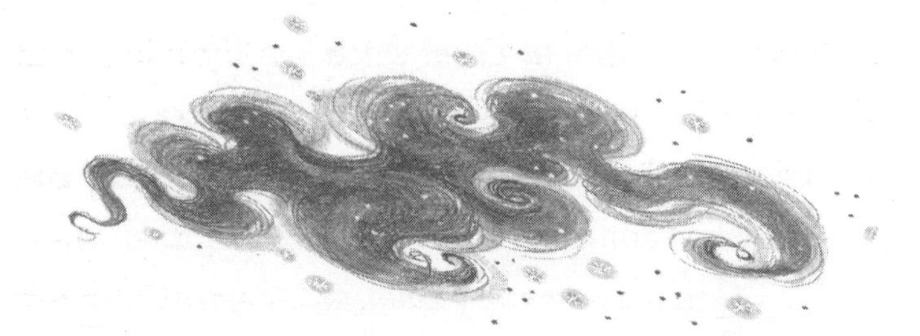

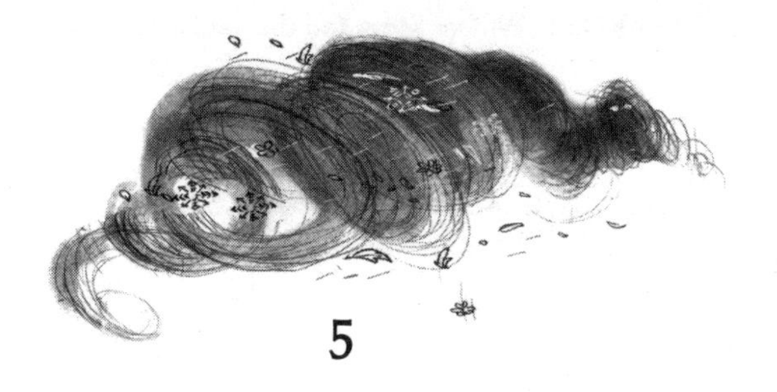

5

The Vision for the Future

'We've got to stop him!' cried Willow. 'We can't let Silas find that staff!'

There was the smallest flash of lightning, and Twist nodded, fast.

'Oi!' called Peg, snapping his fingers. Willow and Twist looked at him in surprise.

'EXCUSE the interruption!' called Master Cuttlefish sarcastically, gaining their attention at last. 'Now that we've finished going over what we learnt last year, and I trust our new students took notes –' he gave them a meaningful look – 'we will make a start on our new curriculum. If you could all turn to the contents page.'

Willow opened the slim blue volume, then blanched. There on the page was everything that they'd feared and *more*.

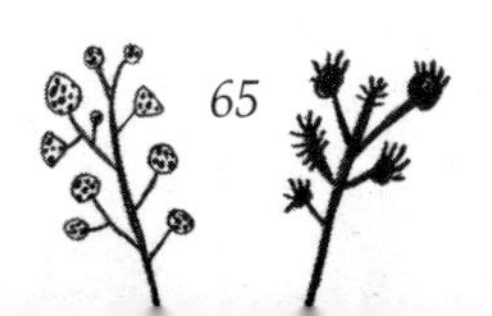

'This can't be right,' breathed Peg.

Willow read on in shock.

Why magic is unnatural

What constitutes a Forbidden area and why we need more of them

What lessons can be learnt from the Long War – and where we went wrong

Why we need to start with magical children first

Magical draining – barbaric or a necessary kindness?

How real unity will begin when we are all exactly the same

The vision for the future: a magic-free world

Willow's eyes were drawn to the words 'Why we need to start with magical children first', and then widened at the perhaps even more ominous ones: 'Magical draining – barbaric or a necessary kindness?'

'This is mad,' said Peg, looking at Willow and Twist.

'Wot? Wot is it?' asked Oswin, his now pumpkin-bright ears inching out of the carpetbag, making a few children gasp in horror.

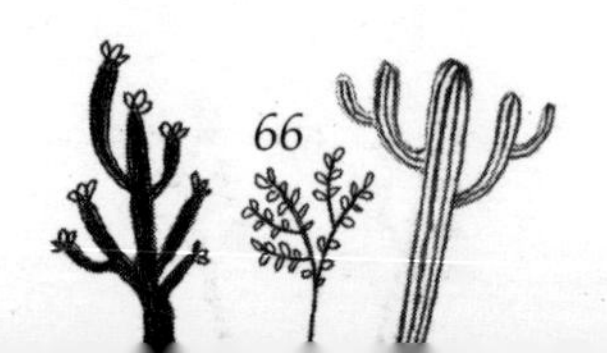

Ignoring them, Willow showed him the book. As the kobold read, his fur turned oddly pale and green, as if he were about to be sick. **'Oh noooo! Oh, me greedy aunt! These cumberworlds is planning on doings us all in! We needs ter skedaddle!'**

'Yes!' said Willow.

'So a kobold is . . . a talking cat?' breathed Twist, momentarily distracted.

Oswin whipped round to glare at her, his eyes turning to angry slits. **'No, they is NOT! I is the monster from under the bed. Or the monster in the bag, or the stove . . . I moves arounds a bit,'** he admitted. **'I is the monster in the room yew is in, when I is in it,'** he decided at last.

Willow shook her head impatiently. 'We don't have time for this, Oswin! We have to get out of here.' Her heart was pounding in her ears.

He nodded. **'Sorry.'**

Peg had started to shout, holding up the book in distaste. 'There's nothing wrong with magical people! This is barbaric!'

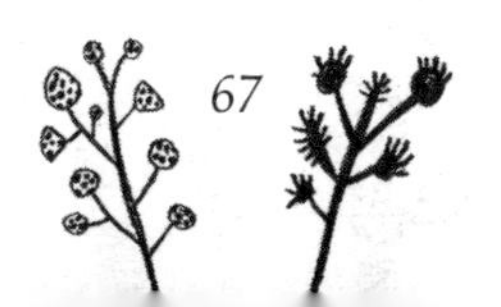

There was a low murmur from the other students. Some, it seemed, like Peg, were also a bit concerned.

'How can we go from lessons on farming to . . . witch-hunting?' asked one.

'What do they mean, "magical draining"? That sounds a bit dangerous. My third cousins have magic. We're not exactly close, but I wouldn't want to actually take their magic away . . .'

Alas, others seemed to think Cuttlefish had every right.

'About time!'

'I always thought they were strange. It makes sense that magic is unnatural.'

Willow had heard enough. 'We're leaving,' she told the teacher, standing up. 'There's no way you'll get away with this.'

To her surprise, Cuttlefish smiled. 'By all means, leave. I'm sure you'll soon have a change of heart, though,' he said, toying with the piece of chalk he'd used earlier to draw an *x* on the classroom door.

Oswin gasped. **'Oh noo! Oh, me greedy aunt! I suspectred somefink fishies. 'E's used Gerful chalk,'** he spat, glaring at the teacher with his large, lamp-like eyes. The kobold had turned a blood-orange colour in

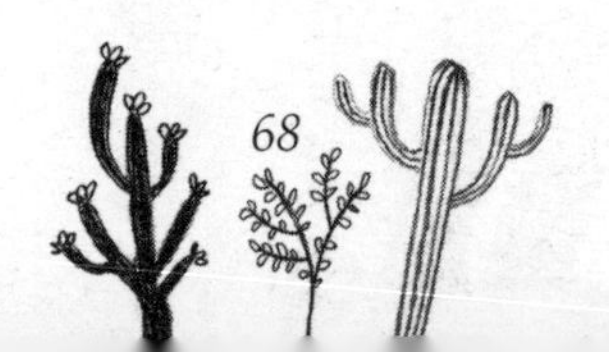

his outrage. **'I knew that pale carbuncle was acting shifties – 'twasn't natural that 'e suddenly found 'is courage. 'E din't! Not till he opened that box!'**

Oswin was speaking about the box from the Brothers of Wol, which had contained the books, as well as the instructions and the mysterious chalk . . .

At Willow, Twist and Peg's confused looks, the kobold explained. **'It controls the mind . . . makes yew believes anyfing someone wants yeh to.'**

The three of them gasped.

Cuttlefish nodded. 'It's nothing to worry about. It's all going to be perfectly fine . . . The Brothers have thought of everything. You see, when you exit through the door marked with the chalk, you won't remember any of your concerns. The chalk puts the mind in a more agreeable, receptive state . . . You'll remember only the lessons we teach you, and you'll be happy about them too. It's genius really.'

Willow gasped. 'That's brainwashing!'

The teacher shrugged. 'Some brains could do with a bit of a wash.'

They stared at him in mute horror.

'You can't drain their magic and think we'll just be okay with that!' cried Peg.

Willow's heart started to thud painfully in her chest. There was a buzzing in her ears and she felt faint. Were they too late? Had Silas already got his hands on the staff?

'That's not happening today, dear boy. The Brothers are working on their cure, which will take some time,' said Cuttlefish. 'It won't be me who performs the miracle. It will be High Master Silas, the new leader of the Brothers of Wol himself. I

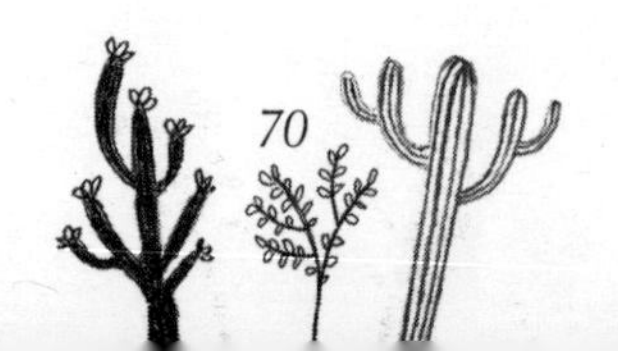

believe he's very close to uncovering the method that will help rid Starfell of this unnatural affliction.'

It took a long while for Willow's breathing to return to normal.

'He hasn't got it yet,' she whispered to Twist, some colour returning to her cheeks.

'Thank Starfell,' breathed Twist.

'It's only a matter of time,' Cuttlefish said, tapping the book. 'But our first goal, really, is to help you to see how important it is that we rid the world of this infection, and that's where *you* all come in . . .' He turned to the rest of the class.

Peg screwed up one green eye as he considered something the others hadn't. 'That's not just for them, is it?' he said, pointing at the chalk **x** on the back of the door. 'It's for all of us, so no one else remembers how wrong this is – otherwise there'd be chaos when the news got out to our parents!'

There was a burst of excitable chatter at this.

'It's for the magical people, Peg, not us,' said the boy called Nigel.

'Not strictly true,' said Cuttlefish, shaking his head. 'Peg is correct. I always knew you were smart, boy. When you all leave class today, things will be a bit hazy, but you'll feel content, as if everything is as it should be.'

'You can't do that!' cried Peg. 'You can't make us all go along with this ... It's madness. Magical people are just different!'

Cuttlefish looked calm as he explained. 'Yes, we can. And we must. You see, the last time we tried to rid the world of magic, the non-magical community showed compassion, tolerance – like you're doing right now, Peg. But the unnaturals preyed on this weakness, and that is why we were never able to stamp out magic. We were weak when we needed to be strong and united. We won't be doing magical folk any favours if we're too soft and let them carry on being diseased when they don't have to be.'

'Diseased!' cried Willow. 'We're not diseased!'

'Yes, yes ... I know *you* believe that, but that is why you're here. We want to help! With this chalk, we will all be on the same side, and over time you'll all come to believe, as you should, that these words are true,' Cuttlefish said, tapping the front of the book again. 'High Master Silas has had a vision about all of this – it's how he was led to the chalk. It is a gift from Wol, bestowed on us so that we can

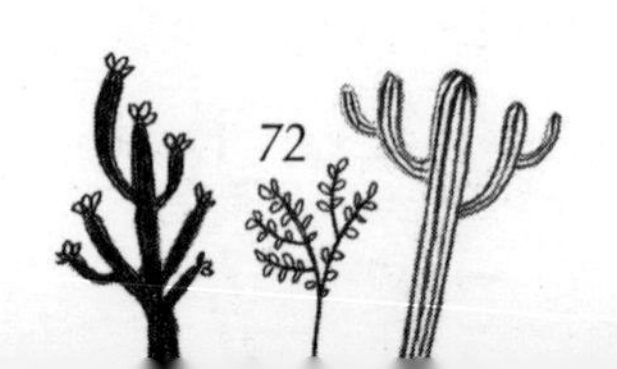

come together at last. Don't you see?'

A few of the children slowly nodded, but Willow was glad to see that a lot of them still looked suspicious and upset.

'Wot a cumberworld. 'E finks it's some kind of miracles. Don' even occur to him 'e's bein' hoodwrinkled – fed some ol' dangerous magic that 'as been med to look like a blesserings,' whispered Oswin.

Willow nodded. She knew Oswin was right. Once again, Silas was using magic and dressing it up as a holy gift.

Then she gasped as she realised something else. She turned to Twist and hissed, 'The grown-ups!' But Twist looked blank. 'The Enchancil meeting – the one about the school plan. That's what must have happened!'

Twist's eyes widened. 'Someone must have used that chalk!' she breathed.

Willow agreed. 'I'm sure of it. Someone has infiltrated the Enchancil. It's why the adults are all suddenly on Silas's side!'

'That makes sense! My aunt said that Celestine Bear was never the type of person who would have just taken the Brothers at their word . . . She thought it was odd.'

Willow nodded. 'And Rubix – it didn't seem like her to just buy into all of that either.'

'They've been brainwashed!'

'We have to get out of here!' cried Twist.

Willow didn't need to consult the StoryPass to know that it was most likely suggesting *'If I Were You, I'd Run'*.

But the chalk on the door presented a major problem. How were they going to get out?

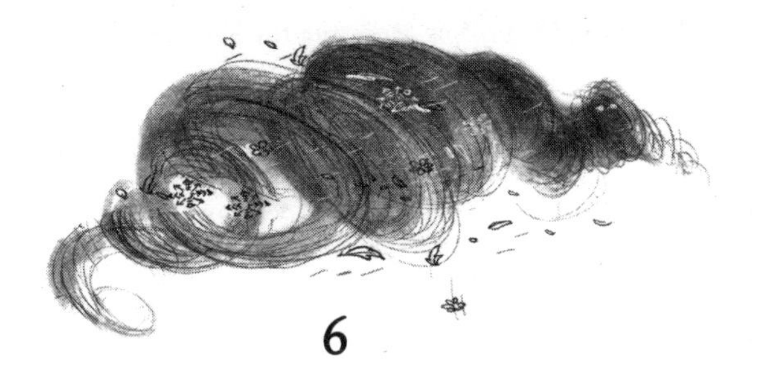

6

Travel by Tornado

'I thought you might say that,' said Cuttlefish, going to his desk and opening up the box on the floor again. 'But I'm afraid I cannot tolerate any more of this disruption. Caraway, Hessan, Gertie and Clementine,' he called.

Willow wondered briefly if these were some kind of weird expletives. But they turned out to be students – the biggest ones – who stood up, looking uncertain.

'I need your help securing our unruly students with these so we can continue our lesson without their magical interference.' Cuttlefish stepped forward with two pairs of iron manacles that were glowing faintly blue.

Willow gasped. She recognised those. They were another of Silas's magical devices, made specifically to lock up witches and wizards – the Brothers of Wol had

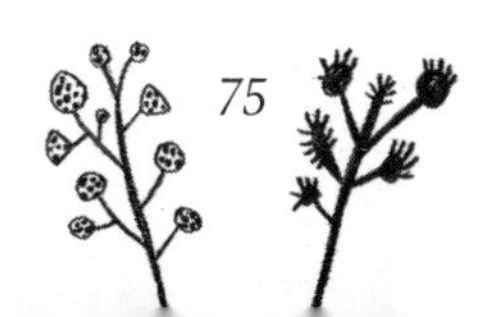

used them to try to seize Moreg Vaine.

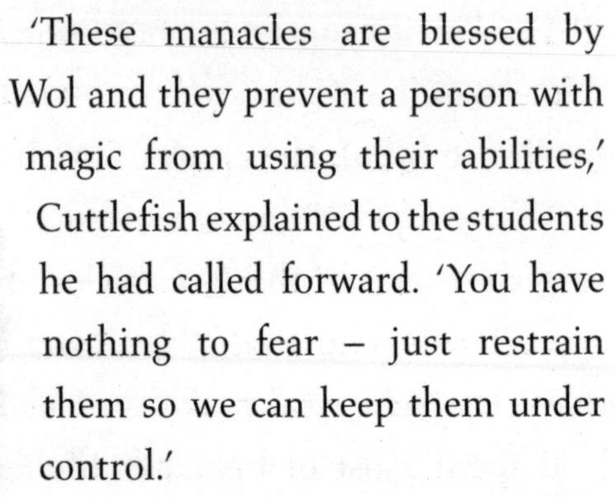

'These manacles are blessed by Wol and they prevent a person with magic from using their abilities,' Cuttlefish explained to the students he had called forward. 'You have nothing to fear – just restrain them so we can keep them under control.'

Caraway, Hessan, Gertie and Clementine looked relieved. Two of them took the manacles and began to advance with determination towards Willow and Twist.

'Those aren't blessed!' cried Willow. 'It's magic!'

'Trust me – it's Wol's blessing,' said Cuttlefish. 'Seize them!'

Willow grabbed her carpetbag, shoved the blue workbook inside and jumped up from her desk. She and Twist leapt away from Cuttlefish and the students – but they were closing in.

Peg dashed towards the door and tried in vain to rub out the chalk.

'Can we try water or something?' asked Twist,

ducking away from one of the approaching students.

The kobold popped his head out of Willow's bag. **'No – won't make no difference. The on'y way is for 'im to break the charm 'imself.'**

The part of Willow's mind that wasn't occupied with the terror of those manacles took a moment to appreciate just how valuable Oswin was at times like these. He had a wealth of knowledge about magic as he'd spent most of his adult life roaming Starfell, looking for a new home after kobolds were banished from their land.

'Can you summon the chalk with your abilities, Willow? Maybe if we have it, we'll be able to break out?' asked Peg, his eyes wild.

Willow shook her head. 'I can only summon it if it's lost! We'll have to get out through the window!'

The trouble was the window was on the other side of the classroom, and she and Twist were cornered! But they could make it if she could just get hold of Whisper . . . She dived towards her broomstick and grabbed it in triumph. She leapt on, Twist scrambling on behind her.

'Stop that this instant!' shouted Cuttlefish, rushing forward and leaping at Twist, knocking her off just as

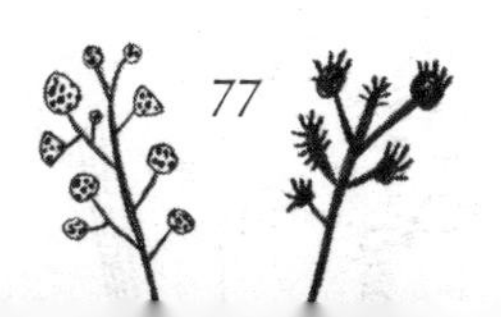

Willow flew towards the ceiling, out of reach.

'Oh no!' cried Willow as Twist stormed towards the teacher, her hair beginning to crackle.

'Don't worry about me!' called Twist. 'I'll be with you in a second.'

Cuttlefish took a step backwards in fear at the look in the elf girl's eyes, before racing after Willow again – perhaps in an effort to get as far away from Twist as possible . . .

Willow swooped down beside Peg, shouting, 'Get on!'

The boy quickly clambered on behind her, his eyes huge.

'Don't you dare take Peg with you! Get back to your desks immediately!' Cuttlefish screeched, again taking a flying leap towards Willow and Peg and managing to claw at the carpetbag.

'Oh noooo! A curse upon yeh,' wailed Oswin, a paw shooting out of the hairy bag to swipe at him.

Cuttlefish roared and held on tighter, despite the sharp pricks from Oswin's claws.

'I'm not sure we'll be able to hold them off!' cried Willow, darting a kick at one of the boys who was trying to pull at her leg, the glowing manacles in his free hand.

The other student with manacles had paused for a moment at the look of fierce revenge in Twist's eyes, but somebody else had bravely stepped forward in an attempt to seize her by the wrist. It was the biggest one, who had a dopy look on his face.

Twist nodded and, as if she were batting off a fly, she managed to fling the boy across the room with a bolt of electrical energy. The others hesitated before coming after her – Twist was obviously very strong – but there were five of them.

In her thunder-voice that made them all shudder, Twist boomed, 'SKIRON!'

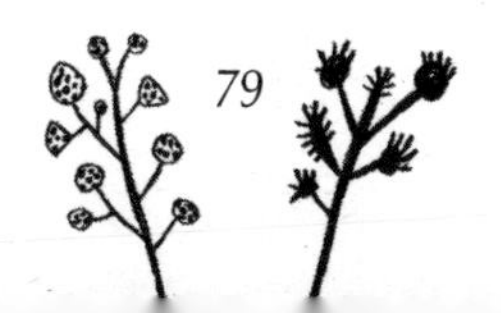

Suddenly the door burst open with a crash and the great icy-blue wind swept into the classroom.

Twist smiled at it the way one would at a beloved but somewhat naughty child. 'Stop them!' she said, pointing to Cuttlefish and the others.

And the wind, which seemed to swell with pride and purpose, lifted the teacher and students into the

air and began to spin them like tops. Wasting no time, Willow aimed Whisper at the row of windows at the back of the classroom. Alas, Skiron's force was so strong that Willow and Peg went flying off course and crashed into the wall. Willow winced as she scraped her arm.

Peg inched his way off the broom, fighting against the strong current, and managed to open the window with some difficulty. There were icicles in his dark hair and his lips had turned blue. Willow held on tightly to her broomstick, steering it firmly towards Peg and battling the gale that threatened to suck Whisper into the same spinning vortex as the teacher and the four students. Peg eventually managed to climb back on.

Twist raced towards them at high speed.

'C'mon, Twist!' cried Willow encouragingly. At last, Twist managed to get a grip on the broom. 'Skiron – let's get out of here!' she shouted, calling the wind that was having a blast spinning Cuttlefish and the students in the air.

Skiron dropped them in a heap on the ground, then gusted towards Willow, Peg and Twist. In a second, it had enveloped them all, and they began to whirl inside the deep blue tornado as it spun out of the window, Peg dangling off the end of the broom by one hand.

Oswin's familiar cries were drowned out somewhat by the howling wind. **'Oh no, oh, me greedy aunt Osbertrude . . . THAT'S ALL THIS FLYIN' STICKS NEEDED . . . A BLIMMIN'**

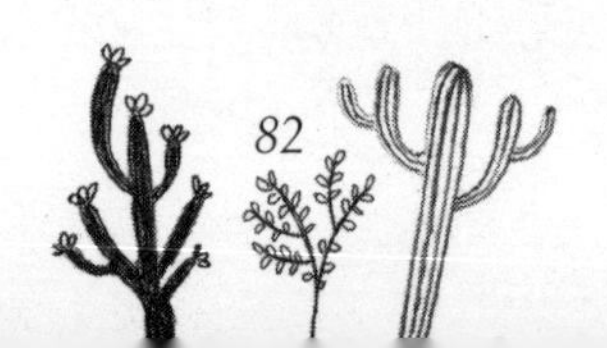

TURBOCHARGE . . . I DON' WANNA DIE AFORE I HAVE THAT STEW!'

If you listened carefully, though, beyond the eerie wail of the wind, you could hear the sound of someone else shrieking. Peg clutched on to the broom for dear life, eyes closed tight, while he yelled, 'OH WOL! MY MOTHER IS GOING TO KILL ME . . . SHE SAID TO STAY AWAY FROM WITCHES, NOT RUN AWAY WITH THEM!'

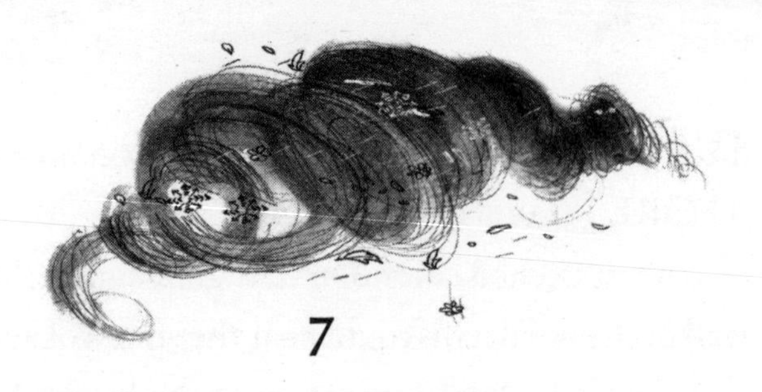

7

The City of Elves

It was early afternoon, and the sun had abandoned its sulk, the sky turning a bright cornflower blue – not that any of them noticed as they flew over the village of Mild at high speed, Peg and Oswin competing in their hollering.

Twist had let Skiron die down now that they were away from the school, but she called out, 'We need to get to Lael as quickly as possible. There's something I have to show you, Willow, and we must tell my aunts what happened at the school so they can get the word out.'

Willow barely had time to ask her what she meant by 'as quickly as possible' before all the air suddenly vanished from her lungs. Skiron had picked up speed, whirling even faster than when they'd left the classroom. Before they knew it, they were shooting

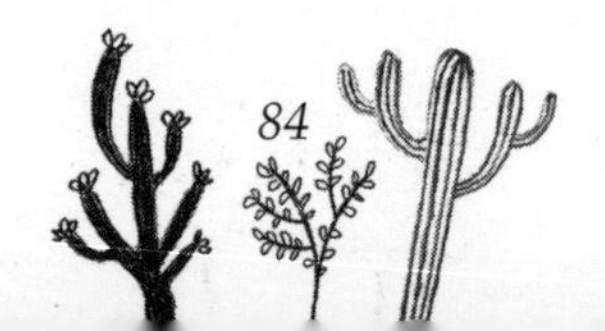

through the air so fast everything turned into a blur.

The wind was icy and cold, and from within the hairy green bag Oswin whimpered, **'Oh noooooooooooooooo. I don' feels wells.'**

Neither did Willow. Ice was forming on the ends of her hair and round her nostrils, and she shivered violently, but she wasn't sure if that was from the cold or from trying desperately not to give in to the nausea.

'I HATE THIS SO MUCH! AAAAAAA-AGHHHHHH!' yelled Peg. 'THIS WILL TEACH ME FOR TRYING TO BE NICE TO NEW PEOPLE!'

They passed streaks of green and blue – forests and lakes that were just blurs to them all – and then, after just moments of being hurtled through the countryside, they arrived outside the tall iron gates of a vast, sprawling city.

And, if the world hadn't been spinning so much, they might have stopped to appreciate how beautiful it was. But it was as if they had just climbed off the longest, fastest rollercoaster in existence, and were now too busy bringing up their breakfasts on a small patch of grass just outside the city walls. Oswin didn't get that far and was sick inside the hairy green bag.

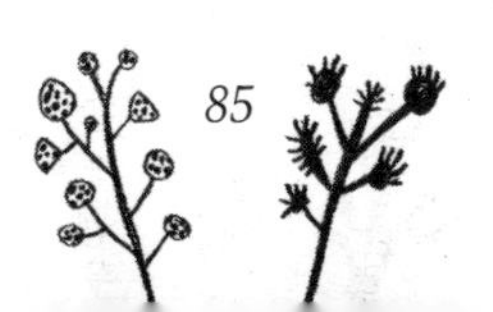

Willow and Peg staggered about as they tried and failed to regain their balance. Peg fell over, only to be sick again. There were spots before Willow's eyes.

Twist looked a little uncomfortable and tried to make a joke. 'I'm sorry. I forget that not everyone is built to travel by tornado.'

No one laughed and the elf looked uncharacteristically awkward.

Willow fought for air as her world continued to spin. Bending over, clutching on to her knees, she whispered, 'It's fine. We'll be all right.'

'Speak fer yerself,' groaned the kobold as he climbed out of the carpetbag. He had turned a very pale green, his furry ears drooping forward. He zipped up the bag with some distaste, then picked it up, giving a small shudder when it sloshed around somewhat. **'This is jes not my day,'** he said mournfully.

'You can say that again,' said Peg. He dry-heaved once more, his head in his hands.

'Water,' said Twist. 'That's what you need.'

Willow nodded. Water would be good. And for the world to just stop spinning . . .

Twist nodded. 'Follow me.'

Willow reluctantly straightened up. And then she

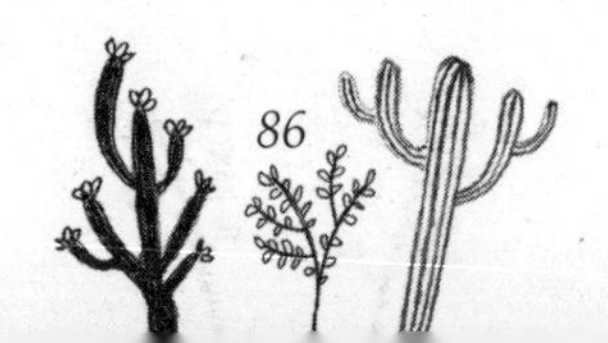

blinked, gasping aloud. She had finally clapped eyes on the vast city before them. Despite the fact that she was still shaken from everything that had happened that morning, she couldn't help marvelling at the sight. 'It's beautiful,' she breathed.

The city wound round a large hill, and everything was made out of white marble, from the tall, polished walls that encircled the perimeter to the intricate houses sculpted from it. They appeared to change colour from palest pink to blue and gold wherever the sun touched them.

'Wow,' said Peg, stopping to take it in, like Willow. 'I've never seen anything like it.'

'I suppose it is pretty,' said Twist, cocking her head to one side and looking at the city critically. Her electrified white-blonde hair listed ever so slightly to the right as she did so. 'I just think of it as home. Funny how you can take things for granted.'

Willow nodded, though a part of her wondered how you could ever get used to something like *this.*

They followed Twist towards the city's entrance, and the enormous pair of blue iron gates sprang suddenly apart as they approached, despite the fact that no one was there to operate them.

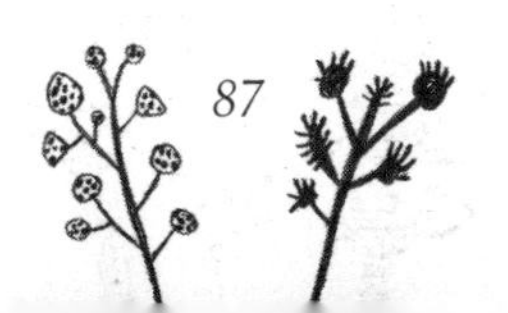

Willow and Peg gasped.

'It's part of the elfsense,' explained Twist as they passed through.

'Elfsense?' asked Willow. She'd heard of it, but never understood it.

Twist nodded. 'It's weird – I've never had to explain it to anyone before. Elves are just born with it, you know? We can sense when another elf is nearby, and we sense other things about each other too – like deceit or when someone is sad.'

'You can read each other's minds?' breathed Peg in shock.

Twist laughed, as if that were absurd. 'No – it's not like that. It's just the surface stuff really.'

'Like thoughts or memories?' asked Willow, thinking of her friend Nolin Sometimes, who, as a forgotten teller, could read other people's memories when he was near them.

'No, it's more about the emotions we feel. We can't tell what another elf is *thinking* exactly, or what might have happened to them, but we'd be able to know how they *felt* about what they were thinking or saying – or sometimes *not* saying . . . Do you know what I mean?'

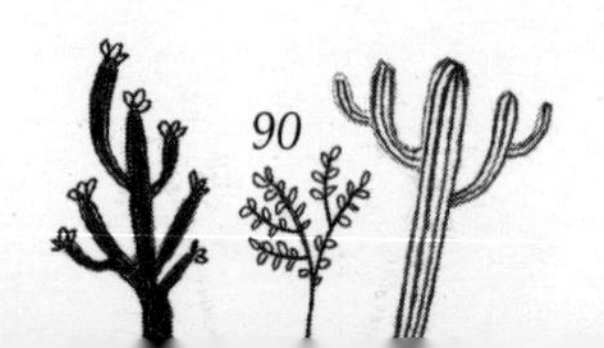

'Mebbe,' said Oswin. **'I can always tell when someone is lyings. Fings turn differents colours.'**

'They do?' said Willow. She knew that Oswin could always spot a lie, just like he could tell when something magical was approaching, but she hadn't known exactly how.

He nodded.

The elf gave him a small smile. 'It's a bit like that for us too. We see emotions as colours, though most of the time we sense a mixture of shades because people tend to feel a mix of things, I suppose.'

Willow frowned as she tried to follow. She realised that it made sense: people often experienced a range of emotions at once. Now she could feel a sense of fear that Silas was close to enacting his plan, anxiety for the magical children across Starfell, plus a bit of guilt for running away from her family again. She still felt slightly ill too, and yet also full of wonder at their beautiful surroundings. Emotions were strange, complicated things.

Twist nodded. 'But it's why we can't hide things from each other as elves, you see? It's what makes elves so direct at times, and it can make us a bit sceptical of humans, as you're so good at hiding what you feel, even from yourselves.'

Willow stared at Twist. She hadn't quite figured out what it was about the elf girl that had unsettled her at first, but now she understood: Twist *was* direct – incredibly so. Initially, Willow had thought that she was just rude . . . She seemed to say things that perhaps you wouldn't normally voice – like, for example, that the person in front of you seemed 'a bit odd'. (*Well, to be fair, pots and kettles,* Willow thought.)

Then there was the fact that Twist had flat-out told Willow that she'd come to find her after reading about her in the paper. Most people would have tried to find a way of making that sound a bit less like they were stalking you . . .

Twist also seemed so capable, so sure of herself – so in charge, despite the fact that she looked like she'd never come into contact with a hairbrush in her life, or an iron. She carried herself as if it were desirable to have hair that electrified around you in a cloud, or clothes that looked like they were put on backwards . . . and somehow it worked.

But Willow didn't think this was arrogance. It wasn't like her sister Camille's inflated opinion

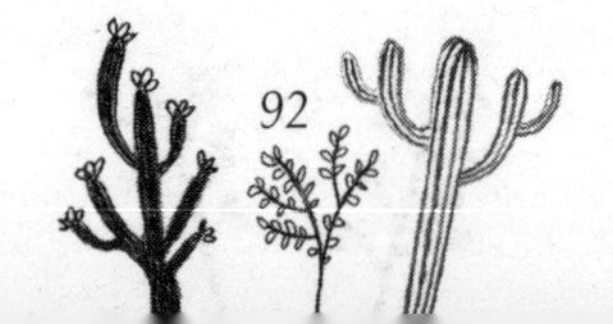

of herself, or the way Juniper acted as if everyone around her owed her something. Twist didn't appear to think she was better than anyone else, or need to make anyone feel less than her – she'd listened to Peg with just as much respect as she had Willow, and she'd done the same with Oswin. She was simply self-assured, with no pretences or disguises. She recognised her abilities and didn't bother trying to hide that she was strong and powerful and capable. She saw no reason to make herself smaller just so that others might feel more comfortable or less frightened. Willow wondered how that must feel – to fully accept yourself, even the wild, odd parts.

Good, she suspected.

'Can't believe I've got to meet an actual elf,' said Peg. 'Or visit Lael. So the whole city is made of marble?' His dark skin had lost its ashen appearance at last, and with his restored health had come his restored curiosity.

Twist grinned at him. 'I haven't met that many humans before – or a kobold! So this is new for me too.'

They all smiled, apart from Oswin, who looked at the carpetbag with a bit of a frown. He wasn't used to walking around in the daylight, but a bag full of sick meant that for once, Willow wouldn't have to carry him.

They followed Twist up a long, winding lane. Even the streets were marble, though different in hue to the houses and walls – a pale blue colour, threaded very lightly with gold. Here and there were trees and plants in polished marbled pots. While Willow's heart was always moved by the wildness of nature, from the colourful forest of Wisperia to the awe-inspiring beauty of the Cloud Mountains, she found she was just as moved by this city of stone. She soon realised why.

'Marble is sentient, you see, as are crystals and other minerals. They're more alive than other materials such as, say, tin or iron, which we find hard to commune with. Some elves can, but marble and crystal are felt best. You see, marble forms part of the elfsense too – it feels what we feel, and it responds. It's been shaped by thousands of elvish hands and minds over the years, and it knows who we are. It will remember us long after we've gone.'

'That's incredible,' breathed Willow.

'Completely,' said Peg, who looked utterly

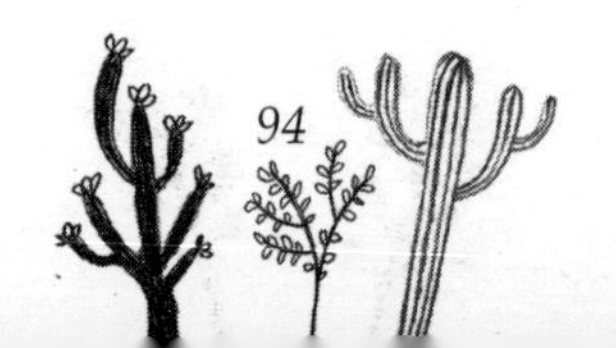

entranced. 'Wow, look at that!' he cried, pointing at a pretty street ahead.

Each of the houses was like a work of art, rounded in shape and topped with a green spire that featured moons or stars. Some of the homes were vast and sprawling, while others were smaller, almost cottage-sized, but each one was finely sculpted out of the pale marble. What was really unique was that each home had some kind of intricate, colourful figure mosaicked into the walls as an adornment, and amazingly they appeared to move as Willow, Twist and Peg neared. Seamlessly skittering across the walls were elves, woodland animals like fawns and rabbits, fire dragons or water nymphs.

'I've never seen houses with moving designs like this before!' said Willow, admiring a life-sized winged horse that seemed to gallop across the walls in shades of blue and green and gold, glowing brightly in the afternoon sun.

'Each home has one – it's a family emblem,' explained Twist. 'It represents the spirit of the people inside. Like this one.' She pointed to a large house that had a stag leaping from one wall to the next. He was blue with dark inky eyes, and, like the others, he was able to move effortlessly across the pale marble walls like a shadow. 'That's the Swift family. They're known for being strong-willed and loyal to a fault.'

Twist then led them up a marble street lined with tall, slim, purple trees.

'And up here is where we live – the Howling family,' she said, pointing to a three-storey marble house with tall blue windows and an unusual spire. The spiralled piece of steel was topped with a crystal orb, framed on each side by a half-moon shape.

But it was the home's emblem that made them all gasp. It was the most wondrous they'd seen yet! It was the profile of a beautiful elvish woman with wild hair floating above her head in shades of white, black, red and brown. Her eyes were closed, and her cheeks were puffed out as she blew several differently hued winds: one that was blue flecked with icy white; an orange one with cascading russet leaves; a green one with swirls of tiny white blossoms; and a golden yellow one . . . All the colours of the winds wound round the house, billowing over the walls as Willow and Peg stared in wonder.

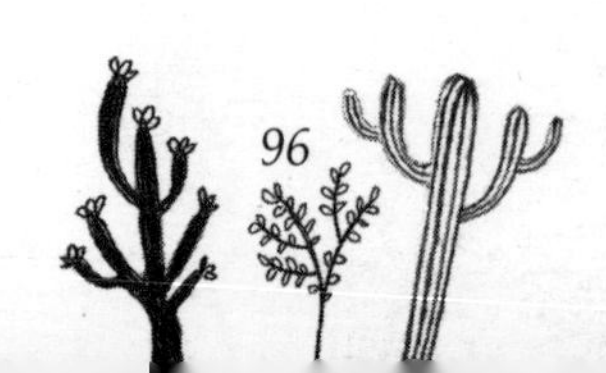

'It's incredible,' breathed Willow, whose heart almost stopped when the figure turned round to look at them and smiled.

'Oh, me greedy aunt,' whispered Oswin.

'She's called Föhn. She represents my aunts and me and the four winds we tame – the north, south, east and west – and their accompanying seasons.'

Föhn blinked a pair of startling green eyes, and then suddenly her mouth opened wide as if she'd taken fright, and she swept away, taking the four colourful winds with her towards the back of the house.

Twist closed her eyes and winced. Then, shoulders drooping, she turned round very, very slowly.

In the distance, there was the sound of thunder and the crackle of lightning. The sky turned dark and grey. The wind began to howl. A heavy storm was brewing . . .

'Trolldash,' said Twist. 'I'd hoped to give you a bit of a breather before *they* came. Sorry.'

'OH NOOOOOOO! Oh, me 'orrid aunt, oh, 'tis the worst day EVER!' cried Oswin.

'What is it?' asked Peg and Willow.

But, before Twist could answer, they saw exactly what it was.

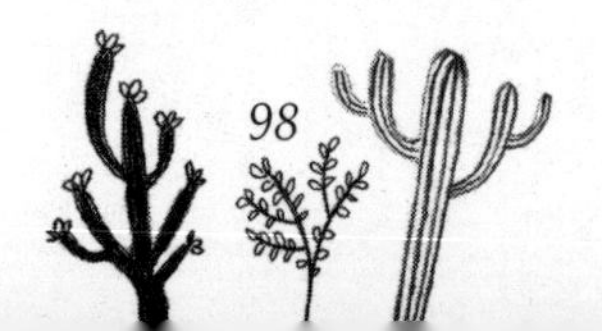

Three tornadoes whirled towards them, and inside each was an older female elf, eyes wild. From their wide-open mouths, they were spewing thunder and rain, and they looked ready to swallow them whole.

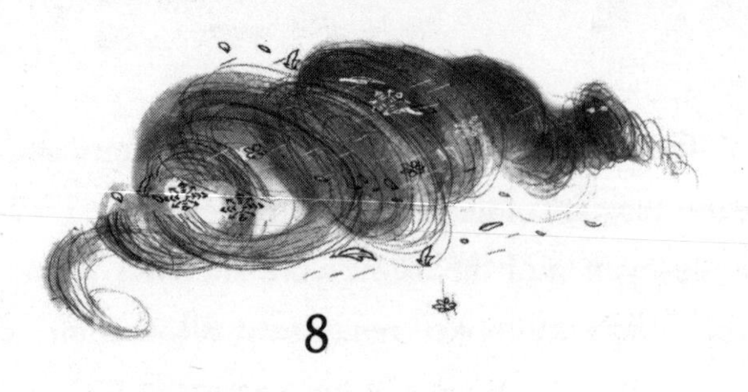

8

The Howling Aunts

Twist sighed as the elves tore towards them. 'I would like to apologise in advance for my aunts,' she said with a grimace.

The force of the aunts' combined wind magic caused Willow, Peg and Oswin to stumble backwards. Rain was falling on their heads and Oswin was trying and failing to cover his fur with his paws.

'Oh nooo, oh, these 'orrid aunts are worser than the worst!'

Wind whipped round their faces, cold then warm, like it was confused, and the sound of the three elvish women speaking at once was deafening. Willow could see why Twist looked momentarily cowed.

'Feeling satisfied, are we?' said one

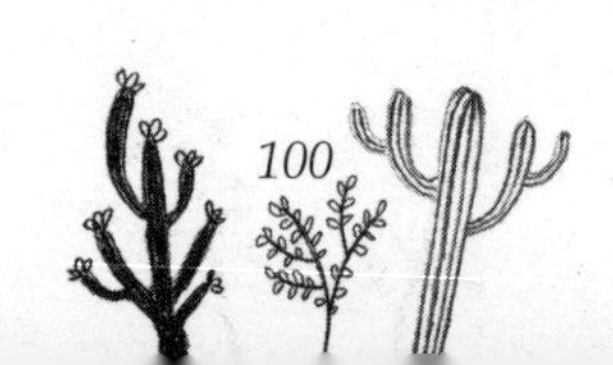

of the aunts. She was shorter than the others, and plump, with a bob of yellow hair.

'I CANNOT BELIEVE you sneaked off EVEN after we specifically forbade it!' said the one with black hair. She was tall and imposing, and wore a long black gown and very sensible shoes.

'Not even a hint of REMORSE!' said the aunt with long, curly red hair and a pair of blue spectacles that twisted up at the corners. She wore a satin and chiffon gown studded with tiny diamantés and shoes that were the very opposite of sensible, with high, slim heels.

They must be using elfsense, thought Willow. Despite what Twist said, it seemed a lot like mind-reading . . . and it didn't seem at all pleasant.

'I sense A LIE TOO,' said the black-haired aunt.

'I sense it too!' the others cried.

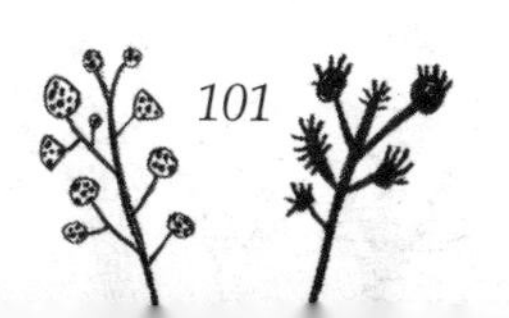

Willow and Oswin shared worried looks . . . What lie?

'It was just a tiny white lie to the teacher. I pretended I had a note,' explained Twist. 'It's the school's stupid rule that you have to bring a note . . .'

'So you crept away, even though you knew that it could be wildly dangerous – that you might even risk losing your magic!' said the black-haired elf.

'YES! It was worth the risk. I had to find out if I was right, and I was, SO THERE!'

There were several booms of thunder and flashes of lightning. The winds howled and Skiron dashed into the fray, twisting with the others – a green one fluttering with blossom and another that was sun-coloured and hazy, like a lake on a hot summer's day.

Willow, Peg and Oswin clapped their hands over their ears at the high-pitched whirring of the winds.

'What did you say?' hissed the aunt with black hair.

'I said, "SO THERE"!'

More shouting, thunder and flashes of lightning ensued.

Skiron gusted into a frenzy, eclipsing all the other winds. Willow, Peg and Oswin held on to each other

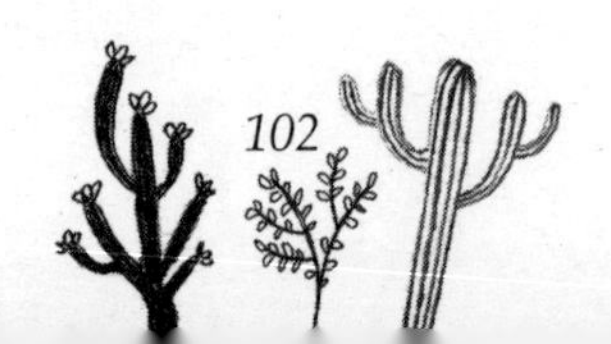

for dear life as the force of the swirling tornado blasted them.

'We don't have time for this.' Twist's pale eyes narrowed, and she looked even fiercer than usual. 'I am going to count to THREE,' she declared.

'HOW DARE YOU?' cried the aunt with black hair. 'I'll FIZZLE you here and now, child!' A bolt of lightning burst out of her mouth and singed the hem of Twist's dress, making Willow, Oswin and Peg jump back in fright.

'Oh nooooo,' whimpered Oswin as he clutched Willow's leg.

Twist was the only one who hadn't moved an inch. Then she smiled, as if her aunt hadn't just tried to burn her to a crisp. 'Well, it was worth a try.'

To Willow's absolute shock, the aunt who had made lightning shoot out of her mouth started to laugh – a great, booming, thundering laugh that was almost as scary as the lightning – and the others soon followed suit. The air stilled as the winds, at last, died down.

'Cheeky miss!'

'Chip off the old gale!'

'Count to THREE. HO HO HO!'

'Just like her mother!'

They all suddenly fell silent at this, their faces sad. 'Couldn't control her either,' said the one with yellow hair, dabbing at her eyes. 'Followed her instincts too!'

Everyone's eyes quickly became misty, including Twist's. 'I'm sorry for making you worry, aunts!' she cried, rushing forward to embrace them.

'Nutters, the lot of 'em. Look wot they did ter me tail,' Oswin sniffed.

Willow saw that the tip was singed. She had to swallow a smile. The kobold was indeed having a bad day. 'Sorry, Os,' she said, giving his head a pat. Showing just how upset he was, he let her.

The aunt that had released a lightning bolt rushed forward to Willow and Peg to introduce herself. 'I'm sorry about all this. I'm Tuppence Howling, one of Twist's aunts. I hope I didn't frighten you too much.' She held out her index finger and touched it to each of theirs, smiling when a small blue spark came from Willow's.

'You mean when you tried to FRY YOUR NIECE? Not at all,' said Peg.

'Don't be silly, boy. If I wanted to fry her, she would just be a pile of ash. I have perfect control over my bolt-ability.' She frowned, her eyes boring into Peg's. 'I resent the accusation.'

Peg recoiled and Willow felt a stab of sympathy for him.

'Really?' muttered Oswin sarcastically. He turned round to show the elf his backside, where, like a griddled steak, two black charred lines had appeared. **'Burnt to a crispid.'** He glared. **'I won' be able ter sit downs fer a week.'**

Tuppence's eyes widened. 'Oh, um . . . I'm really sorry.'

Willow and Peg fought hard not to laugh. Peg didn't win. The kobold glared at the boy, who bit his fist to hide his chuckles.

The aunt then peered more closely at Oswin and gasped. 'Why, you're a kobold!'

'Mebbe,' said Oswin, glaring at her from between Willow's legs. **'Who's askin'?'**

'My goodness, you really are. I thought you'd all but died out, I mean apart from—' At Oswin's glower, Tuppence broke off and frowned. 'Never mind.'

Twist introduced the rest of them. 'So you've met Tuppence. This is Griselda –' she gestured to the aunt with red hair and glasses – 'and Dot.' She pointed out the aunt with yellow hair. 'Aunts, this is Willow Moss.'

'Oh!' they all gasped. 'So you found her.'

'I did,' said Twist.

As Griselda opened her mouth to say something else, Twist held up a hand. 'I know there's a lot to discuss – but right now it can wait. They all need some water and a sit-down. I, er, gave them a lift over . . .'

'Ah, poor mites. Lost their breakfasts?' asked Dot.

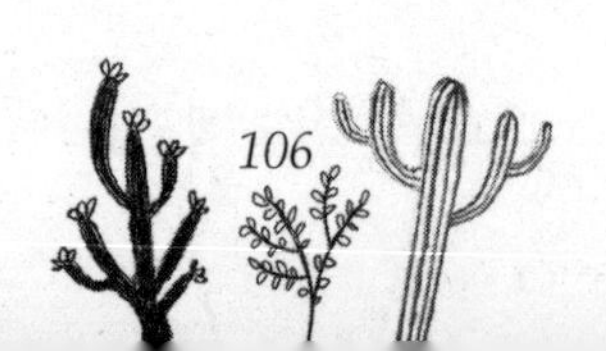

'Every bit,' said Twist, who didn't seem all that sorry about it. She turned to Willow, Peg and Oswin. 'Follow me. I'll get you that water, and then we'll tell my aunts about what we found out. Because we're going to need their help.'

'More than just ours, if you've been proven right, Twist,' said Tuppence.

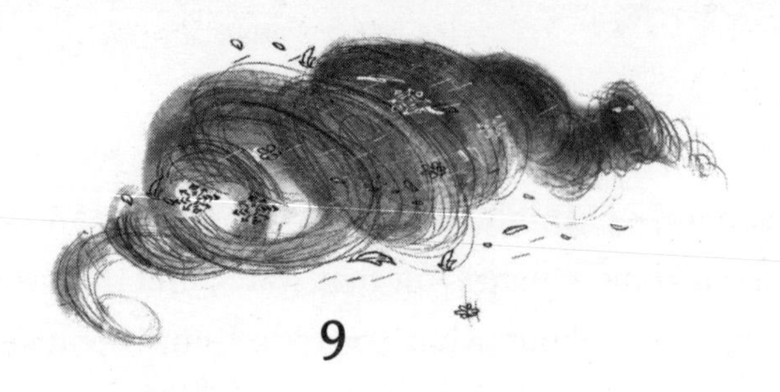

9

The House That Seemed Alive

Willow and the others followed after the elvish women as they marched towards the marble house. The wide blue doors flung themselves open.

'Selia,' said the elves together, and each of the winds stayed outside.

The elvish home was every bit as beautiful inside as out. The hallway was marble too, in shades of palest blue and green.

Willow's own home was cluttered with tables, chairs and shelves crammed with books, teacups, old potions and things from her mother's Travelling Fortune Fair. (These included crystal balls, gauzy shawls and black candles, which people believed helped Raine to commune with the dead . . . None of them made a difference, but they were all part of the 'ambience', as her mum said – or, as Willow privately

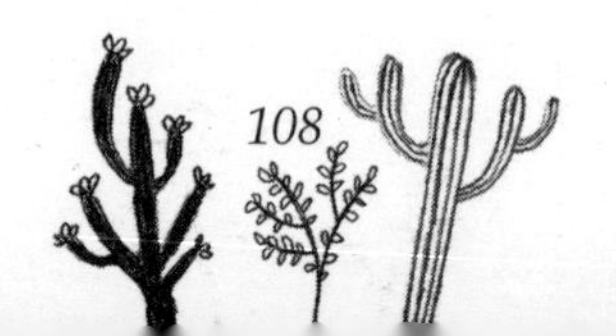

thought, helped to 'drive the price up'.)

Unlike Moss Cottage, Howling House was wide, open and airy, with the occasional gilded table in the corner or plant in a pot, a few of which seemed to be opening their eyes to get a better look at them. There was a large green sofa piled with cushions and, just as Twist was directing them to it, a small marble sidetable with gold chicken legs came scurrying towards them. It was topped with several glasses of water.

Willow's mouth fell open.

'Thanks, Scratch,' said Twist, handing the glasses round.

'That table has feet!' cried Peg.

'Yours don't?' asked Griselda, flicking back her long red curls as she arranged herself on one of the velvet couches, high heels dangling over the side.

'Er, no,' said Peg.

'Mmm, humans are strange,' said Dot. 'I'm not sure I could live in a dead house.'

'A dead house?' asked Willow.

Dot paused. 'One without thought or feeling. Scratch is part of this place, like the bathrooms or doors, and they all respond to our needs.'

'Is it like . . . a charmed house?' Willow asked, thinking of Rubix's star-shaped home, Pimpernell's tower or even the wizard Holloway's copper boat, *Sudsfarer*.

'Well, yes, in a very crude way,' said Tuppence.

At the same moment, Griselda snorted, 'Not at all! Charms are a bit vulgar, if you ask me.'

'Sisters, don't be rude,' said Dot with a motherly sort of smile that revealed the dimples in her round face. She rolled her eyes at Peg and Willow. 'It's rather a touchy subject,' she confessed. 'A charm is a kind of awakening. The witch who performs it searches for the small fragments of soul that exist within the material, lying dormant. The difference with elfsense is that our homes and objects are never forced to awaken – they simply begin to respond out of choice. Do you follow?'

Willow and Peg frowned, and Tuppence tried to explain as Dot hurried off to the kitchen.

'When something is charmed,' said Tuppence, 'it's cajoled and flattered into doing something it wouldn't usually do.'

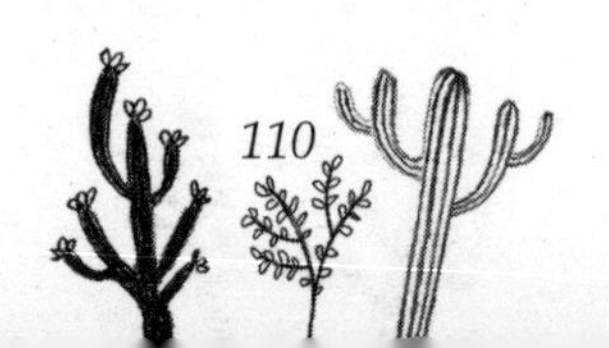

'So it doesn't want to be charmed?' asked Willow.

'I wouldn't say that,' said Griselda, pushing up her rhinestone glasses. 'It's a charm because it has found the witch who uses it charming.' She grinned and they all grinned back.

'The charmed object doesn't mind, but it isn't exactly behaving naturally,' said Tuppence, pushing her sister Griselda's high-heeled feet off the couch and giving her a hard stare.

Griselda gave a dramatic sigh, then sat up straight. 'My feet are sore,' she complained.

Tuppence raised a dark eyebrow and gave Griselda's heels a pointed look.

Griselda muttered, 'It's not always sensible to be sensible, especially when it comes to pretty shoes . . . Something you'll never understand.'

Tuppence turned back to Willow, ignoring her sister. 'Elvish marble or crystal, on the other hand, comes alive of its own free will. And, when an elf wants to build a house, they have to wait for the right stone. You can't just go to a quarry or a mine and choose what *you* like.'

'You can't?' said Peg, surprised.

'Well, you could, but then the house would never

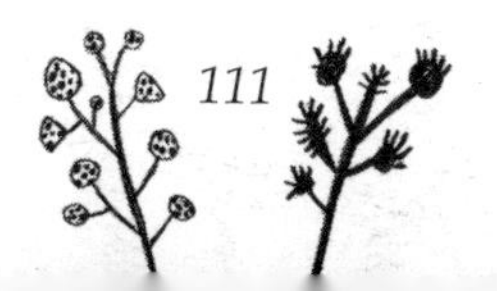

respond to you,' said Dot, reappearing with a plate of strange-looking fruit. She was followed closely by Scratch, who was piled high with all manner of vegetable snacks and dips.

'How do you know which is the right marble?' asked Peg.

Dot offered around the plate of weird fruit. 'Whirlhip?' It was bright purple with red seeds, and as Willow bit into hers, she gasped. It was sweet and slightly spicy, with an almost cinnamon and honey taste.

'When a material like marble or crystal chooses you, it changes colour beneath your fingers,' Dot said, putting the plate on Scratch's surface. She reached down to touch the marble floor, which began to glow a faint green. 'See? That's when you know it wants to be yours too – and that it enjoys its role. Only a house that likes its occupants will anticipate their needs and help their guests too.' Dot gave Scratch a pat, and it wriggled a bit from side to side like a dog wagging its tail.

'Why is Lael made mostly of marble then?' asked Peg. 'If other materials can respond the same way?'

'Well, marble is easier to obtain. The vanished kingdom was mostly made of crystal, so I've heard, but nearly all the crystal mines are exhausted now . . .'

'And iron isn't exactly pretty,' added Griselda. Tuppence rolled her eyes, but Griselda shrugged. 'What? It's true.'

Elf houses seemed incredible. Willow couldn't imagine what it must be like to simply voice a need and have her house try to cater to it. She had a sudden, wild vision of a toilet running after her and had to stop herself from laughing out loud . . . She wasn't sure about *that.*

'Fascinating as all this no doubt is to our guests,' interrupted Twist with her customary directness, 'they aren't here on a social call. Like I said earlier, aunts, it's as I feared. The Brothers of Wol have only let magical children into their schools because they plan to strip them of their magic.'

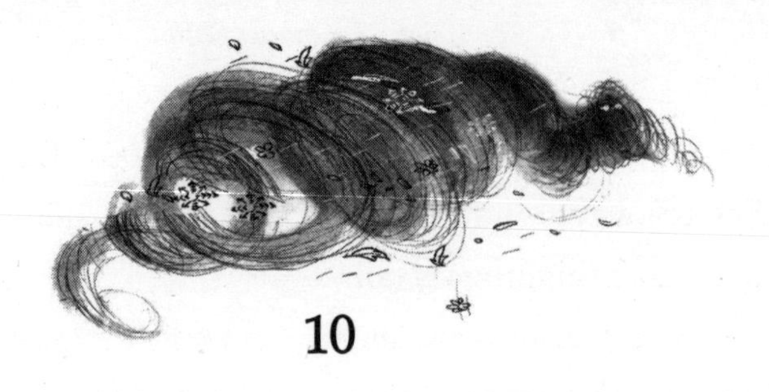

10

The Consequences of Magic

Twist's words caused an air of seriousness to descend on the room.

'Oh Wol, no!' cried Tuppence.

'Does he have the elf staff already?' wailed Griselda.

'Has he found the vanished kingdom?' exclaimed Dot.

'No,' said Twist, 'not yet . . . but that's his plan, I'm sure of it.'

'That's what the queen's staff was called? The elf staff?' asked Willow, and Twist nodded.

'What's a staff got to do with anything?' asked Peg, thoroughly confused. 'I don't remember Cuttlefish saying anything about that.'

'Remember he said that Silas was working on a "cure"? A way to strip magic from people?' said Twist. 'Well, we think we know how he's going to do

it – and it involves an ancient staff that once belonged to us elves.'

Everyone gathered round a dining table as Twist filled Peg in on the long-lost elvish kingdom, the stolen scroll containing the queen's last words and how, shortly after the theft, Silas amended the treaty to allow mixed schooling.

'And, as we've found out, they're planning to take away children's magic. It all adds up – Silas stole that scroll, and now he's after the staff.'

Tuppence looked nonplussed. 'So this teacher just *told* you that they're planning on removing children's magic?'

They nodded.

Willow produced the small workbook that she'd taken from the school, anticipating moments like this when proof might be needed, and handed it over. The aunts passed it around, each one clutching their chest and gasping as they read what the Brothers of Wol planned to teach children.

'B-but that's ludicrous!' cried Dot.

'And utterly foolish too, on his part – considering that everyone will now know their plan. I mean,' Tuppence said, holding up the small book, 'why advertise the fact that they want to rip away children's magic? Why tell everyone?'

'Because they is using Gerful chalk,' said Oswin.

The aunts gasped.

'We had to break out of the classroom window. The teacher marked the door with the chalk, and if we'd gone that way . . . well,' said Willow, clenching her jaw, 'we would have been fooled into believing that this was all a good idea.'

Dot glared at Twist. 'You see now why we didn't want you to go? Look what might have happened! You could have been brainwashed – and taken somewhere to have your magic stolen!'

Twist glared back. 'It *is* happening . . . This is his plan. That's why I needed to go – to team up with Willow, who's been right all along. I'm glad I did because now there's a chance we can stop him. But we can only do that by helping – not by staying home, not by burying our heads in the sand or pretending everything's all right!'

Dot stared at Twist, then sighed, her face downcast. 'You're right.' She looked at her niece with new respect laced with sadness. 'I wish I could keep you safe at home, though.'

Twist's eyes softened. 'I know that, Aunt Dot.'

Willow looked at them. 'It wasn't just Gerful chalk our teacher had. He also had manacles that had been magicked. The non-magical folk have been told that all these things are "blessings from Wol" – and they seem to believe it. I wonder how many Brothers of Wol even know the truth about Silas and just how dangerous he really is.'

'Hang on,' said Peg, standing up. 'Were those things really *magic*? And what do you mean, "the truth about Silas"?'

Willow blew out her cheeks. 'Silas is a wizard.'

Peg sat back down with a thud. 'Now I've heard it all.'

'Yew tellings me,' said Oswin.

'A wizard?' repeated Peg. Then he looked at them all sceptically. 'Are you sure about that? I mean . . . it just doesn't make any sense. AT ALL. The Brothers of Wol are *against* magic. Aren't they trying to "cure" it?'

'I know it seems that way, but that confusion is what Silas is relying on so no one suspects him,' said Willow. 'But it's the truth – Silas was born with magic.' She filled them in on everything that she'd discovered. 'He was brought up in Wolkana with the Brothers of Wol and didn't know who his parents were. So, when he developed a fizz of magic, he was raised to be ashamed of who he was. They told him to pray for it to be taken away.'

Peg wasn't the only one who winced at the idea.

'It was only many years later that he found out that he was the High Master's son and that his mother was a witch. In fact, he's the nephew of one of the greatest witches alive, Moreg Vaine.'

'No!' cried the aunts in shock.

'You can't be serious!' gasped Twist.

Even Peg looked surprised. 'Oh Wol! I've heard of her . . . Doesn't she pickle children in ginger and have tea parties with the dead?'

''Tis jes rubbish mostly,' admitted Oswin. **''Cept the tea parties. Thems is real. Though they is not much of a party – more like a visits to a nightmare where yew coulds lose yer soul. We all went actually,'** he added brightly.

Peg and the aunts blinked at him.

'Um, anyway,' said Willow, who didn't think that now was the time to explain Netherfell to poor Peg, 'Silas's mother died when he was a baby, so Moreg left him with his father, the High Master, to be raised by the Brothers of Wol.'

'Why on Great Starfell would she have left a baby – who, with a bloodline like the Vaine family, stood a good chance of having magic – with the Brothers of Wol?' cried Dot, who had gone pale.

'Surely she must have known how he'd be raised!' cried Tuppence. 'I've always thought of her as shrewd, a few steps ahead, but never . . . cruel.'

Willow shook her head, her face flushing slightly as she felt herself prickle with defensiveness. Moreg was many things – practical, quirky, slightly off her rocker, yes . . . but not cruel. Besides, she did nothing, nothing at all, without a reason. However, Willow could understand the aunts' confusion. She had asked

Moreg about this herself the last time she'd seen her – before Moreg disappeared.

Willow had opened the cottage door in surprise to find the witch staring back at her – impossibly tall, with the ability, somehow, to make someone's knees decide to take an impromptu holiday.

'Cup of tea?' she'd suggested. It was the same thing the witch had said to her the first day she'd shown up on Willow's doorstep and decided to change her life forever.

Willow had smiled, then fished out her StoryPass. The dial was currently suggesting a cup of tea too.

Moreg had taken a seat at Willow's scrubbed wooden table, a cup of hethal tea in her hands, and looked at her with eyes like razors. 'I know what you're thinking,' she'd said.

Willow was startled. There was, after all, a rumour that the witch could read minds – a rumour Willow had tried to ignore.

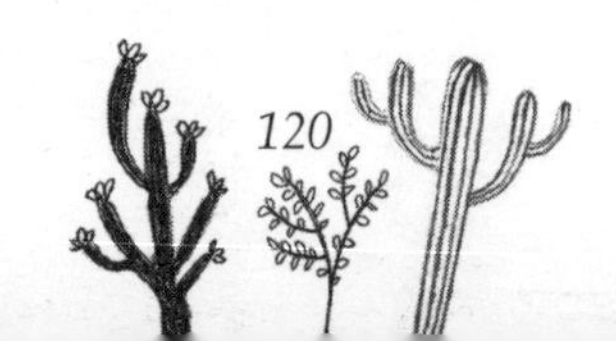

But Moreg had continued, 'Because I've been thinking it too. Ever since we got back from Netherfell, I've been asking myself, why? Why does Silas want to steal everyone's magic? Why does he feel the need to be all-powerful?'

Willow had nodded. 'It's like he hates magical people – which doesn't make sense to me because he's magic himself. After he realised he was lied to by his father, why wouldn't he have just come over to our side?'

Moreg looked at the floor. 'I think because it happened too late. They'd already convinced him that magic was unnatural, that it was a curse . . . And that's my fault. I never would have placed him there if I'd known what was going to happen.'

'So, erm, why *did* you leave Silas with the Brothers?'

'When I discovered that my sister had died, I should have raised her baby myself . . . And I would have done. But I had a vision – I saw things changing. I saw Silas with the Brothers, as a new leader. I saw him wielding *magic*. I thought that I was seeing a happy vision of the future, Willow . . . not this. Never this. I hope you'll believe me.'

'Of course I do,' Willow had cried.

'You see, I made the mistake of projecting my own

hopes into the visions I was having. I believed, naively, that if the High Master realised that his own son had magic, it might put an end to this animosity between the communities. That if he could see that there was nothing to be afraid of, it would pave the way for peace. I thought perhaps we were halfway there, considering he'd already fallen for my sister – but, of course, it didn't work that way.

'The High Master liked Molsa *in spite* of the fact that she was a witch. He wished that she didn't have that "affliction", and Silas was raised to be ashamed of that part of himself – as if it were something he could simply wish away. When Silas found out that he was my nephew and that I didn't take him in – didn't spare him that pain and suffering – well, I think he felt rejected not just by me, but by the entire magical community.

'He has become so twisted. He knows he's been lied to, yet he still believes what he's been taught – that magic is unnatural. But then, of course, he found out the hidden truth about Wol – that the "god" they'd worshipped all along was in fact a wizard too, like him. So Silas decided to do what Wol tried and failed to achieve – to rid every last living creature

within Starfell of magic, and in the process take all that magic for himself. To become something else, something more – like a god.

'If I've learnt one thing about human nature, Willow, it's that we all see the world though our own imperfect lens – myself included – and so a seer's vision of the future is clouded by that, becoming imperfect and subjective too. I regret my decision to give up Silas, but I did what I thought best at the time. In life, we may only move forward, looking back only to help navigate the way. What we must do now is stop him.'

Before Moreg had left, the witch's eyes had turned white for a moment as she experienced a vision, then back to black. She'd said, 'You might want to fish that whistle out from under your bed. Who knows when you'll need to summon a troll army?'

Willow had blinked. She'd forgotten all about the troll whistle. She'd been given it some time ago by the troll chief while trying to find the missing Tuesday.

It had now been months since Willow had seen Moreg, but she had carried the troll whistle in her bag ever since.

Willow explained everything that Moreg had told her. Even now, after all this time, after Moreg hadn't come forward to clear Willow's name or put things right, Willow still believed in her.

'This can't be right!' said Peg, standing up again, his hands in his hair. 'Someone would have known. Someone would have stopped him!'

'We've tried – but look at the trouble he's gone to,' Willow said. 'Remember the chalk! It's like no one can think for themselves, so he's just getting away with it . . . But he won't. Not if we stop him, and we will somehow.'

Peg shook his head. 'I feel like my head's spinning. This is a . . . lot to take in.'

Dot came forward and touched his arm. 'We could take you home. Would you like that?'

Peg looked from Willow to Twist and the aunts, then shook his head slowly. 'No. I don't know . . . This is scary, I won't lie. But, if I went home, I couldn't pretend that this was okay . . . Like Twist said, I feel I should do what I can. I may not have magic, but maybe I can help somehow.'

'If you're sure?' asked Twist.

Peg nodded. 'I'm good at one thing – puzzles,

logic. It might help.'

Willow nodded, remembering that it was Peg who'd figured out that the Gerful chalk wasn't just for the magical children – that it would be used on everyone. 'Practical makes perfect,' she said, using one of Moreg's favourite phrases.

Peg cocked his head to the side, confused. But the elves all nodded.

'Oh yes,' said Tuppence. 'Solving something without magic – well, that's sometimes the hardest and most valuable form of power there is.' She stood up, taking the booklet that Willow had shown them. 'I'll take this, if you don't mind. I think we'll be doing the rounds with it, trying to get the word out to the magical community.'

'I'll go to Dwarf Territory. If the Brothers are using Gerful chalk, we'll need dwarfish dust. It protects against mind control,' explained Griselda.

'Good thinking,' said Dot. 'I'll go with Tuppence, and you lot can come with us.'

'No,' said Twist. 'I have to show Willow the mural. Then I need her to try to find the vanished kingdom!'

Pandemonium ensued.

At the aunts' cries, their winds whipped inside the house to investigate, stirring up a trail of leaves, blossom and ice. It began to rain, then snow, then autumn leaves fell from nowhere, followed by a warm summer breeze – all in seconds.

'It's all right, Skiron!' cried Twist.

The aunts called out to their own winds too, each giving the command for them to scatter outside again: *'Selia!'*

Peg wrung out his wet shirt, muttering, 'I don't know how I'll ever explain any of this.'

'You can't ask Willow to summon a whole kingdom! It would be madness – you don't know what mayhem you could cause!' cried Griselda.

'An earthquake!' gasped Dot.

'Or an avalanche, or a tsunami . . . People could die!' breathed Tuppence.

'I didn't think of that,' said Twist, who looked stricken.

Willow had to admit that very, very distantly, a tiny pebble-like idea had been rolling around in the back of her mind. She'd been wondering

about whether it would be possible to simply *find* the kingdom using her magic . . . considering that it *was* lost.

But, thankfully, she had learnt one lesson from trying to find a missing day: magic wasn't something you could simply play with. There were consequences to forcing something to reappear.

'I agree,' said Willow. 'I think if I were to bring the kingdom back – and I'm not saying for sure I *can* – we'd need to first know where it's been this whole time, if that makes sense. You can't just summon something back and not expect there to be consequences. Things don't vanish to nowhere – they're always *somewhere*, and you've got to negotiate how you bring them back or things could go . . . wrong. Catastrophically wrong. For example, if a lost book is under someone's bed, buried under a pile of socks, it won't matter too much if I summon it. Maybe the sock pile will just rearrange itself a bit. But who *knows* what could happen if I summon a whole kingdom?'

Twist's and Peg's eyes were huge.

'I hadn't thought of that,' admitted Twist.

'Well, at least Willow has,' said Tuppence. 'That's reassuring.'

Willow nodded, but she didn't explain that she'd

learnt that lesson the hard way . . . When she'd been on the verge of summoning back the missing day with her magic, Moreg had stopped her just in time. Apparently, if she'd done it, she could have unravelled the fabric of Starfell itself – and *ended the world.*

Sometimes it was best to quit while you were ahead, especially when people were starting to think you were smart.

Then Willow had a new thought . . . She closed her eyes for a moment and raised her hands to the sky.

'What are you doing?' cried Peg. 'You just said—'

Willow opened one eye. 'That I couldn't summon a whole *kingdom* without consequences, yes. But a staff? Well, that might not be so bad.'

'Oh! Good thinking!' cried Dot.

'Go on then,' said Tuppence.

Willow closed her eyes and tried to focus. With her particular skill, she was used to having an audience, as her customers lined up outside the cottage door every morning, looking for her help to locate their missing possessions. But there wasn't usually so much *pressure.*

She took a deep breath, put Twist and her aunts out of her mind and began to search.

There was something there, but the more she pulled, the more she met resistance. She tried once more – and was suddenly pushed back with such force it was as if she'd touched an electric current. She landed spread-eagled on the marble floor, and a deluge of briny water and several lengths of seaweed fell from nowhere and landed in her still-outstretched hands.

Willow opened her eyes and sighed, looking like a drowned rat. 'Well, it was worth a try. It's under some kind of heavy protection.'

Tuppence and the aunts nodded. 'That makes sense,' sighed Griselda.

There was a skittering sound as Scratch came hurrying towards Willow with a towel, a dustpan and brush and a mophead on its tabletop.

'Thanks,' Willow said, taking the towel. Scratch began sweeping up the scattered leaves from the aunts' magic, and then quickly mopped the floor. She was bemused when afterwards it began picking seaweed from her hair with its chicken-like feet. When it had finished, it edged towards Oswin, who scurried out of its way, the carpetbag in his arms. The table drummed a foot as if it were impatient, and then backed away.

'Well, we learnt one thing from that at least,' said Willow.

'Wot?' asked Oswin. **'Tables can use their feet to combs 'air?'**

She grinned. 'Not that. Wherever the staff is, it's underwater and protected, which means I don't think Silas has it yet.'

They all breathed a sigh of relief. That *was* good news.

'But there's a lot riding on that "yet",' said Tuppence, standing up. 'We don't have time to lose. There must be hundreds of scared children out there and we need to act quickly.' She put her hands on Twist's shoulders. 'You were right – and we should have trusted your instincts. But please, please be careful.'

Twist nodded. 'We will.'

Griselda stood too, wincing in her high heels. 'Send a raven if you need us.'

Tuppence looked at her. 'Oh, for Wol's sake! Change your shoes, you vain elf.'

Griselda straightened her long, beautiful gown and pushed up her rhinestone spectacles. 'I'd rather make an impression,' she said, then winked at the girls.

Willow couldn't help grinning back.

They watched the aunts as they departed through the open door in their whirling tornadoes of gold, orange and green, and then Twist turned to Willow.

'Come on – I need to show you the wall. It's trying to tell me something . . . I just don't know what.'

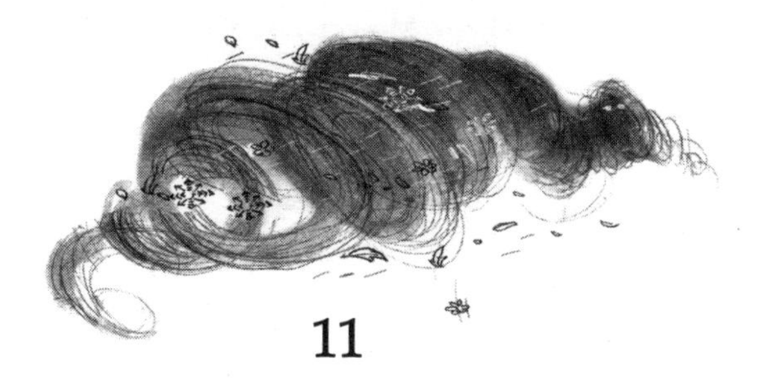

11

The Mural

'A wall is trying to tell you something?' Peg frowned, then shook his head. 'Actually, after everything I've seen today – including pictures that move on houses, elves who can practically read minds, as well as command the wind and make lightning come out of their mouths – well, sure. Why not? Why wouldn't a wall be talking to you?'

They all started to laugh as they headed out of Howling House.

'It is a bit mad,' admitted Willow. 'I've never seen anything like it either.'

Peg laughed even harder. 'And you're magic!' Which set them all off again.

When they had at last recovered, Twist shook her head and gave a wry grin. 'I meant the mural. It's on a wall in the city centre.'

'Oh,' said Willow, remembering that Twist had said something about a mural earlier. 'What is this mural?'

'It's how I worked out the secret about Queen Almefeira's staff – the fact it could take away magic. You see, it's not just *any* old mural. It was created in marble a thousand years ago by the descendants of the queen, soon after the old kingdom vanished. You know how elvish marble will only respond to the one family it chooses?'

They nodded.

'Well, this mural responded to *me*.'

Willow was frowning, not quite putting the two facts together, but Peg got there first.

His mouth fell open as he gasped, 'You're royalty! It responds to you because you're the queen's family too?'

Oswin's and Willow's mouths also flew open in shock.

'Wot?' cried Oswin.

Twist nodded, but waggled her hand in a 'sort of' motion. 'Yes. But very, very distantly. I mean, it's not recognised today. No one's going to bow when any of us go past – elves are governed by an elected body

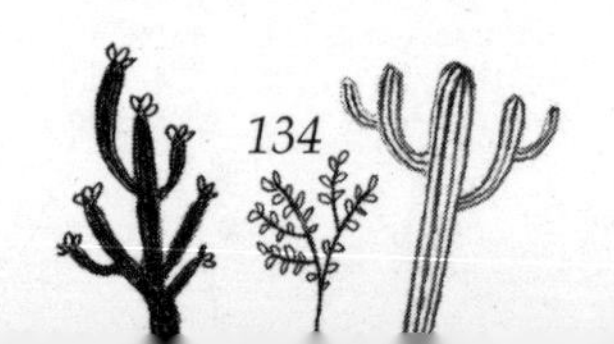

nowadays. But, yes, my aunts and I are elvish royalty *technically*.'

'Wow,' said Willow.

'I'll say,' agreed Peg.

There was a sound of scrabbling feet behind them, and they turned to find that Scratch the table had followed them outside. It started circling Oswin in a very determined way, as the kobold yelped, **'Oi, stop that! Get away from me.'**

But the table ignored him and made a dash for the hairy green bag at Oswin's side. It managed to slide the bag on to its tabletop and scurry quickly away, on its long chicken legs, back inside Howling House.

'Oi! Yew cumberworld, that's mine! Come back!' hissed Oswin.

'Don't worry. He's just going to clean it,' said Twist. 'He'll bring it back. Scratch has a heightened sense of smell.' Then she gave a wry smile. 'For something without a nose.'

'I'm not sure you need a heightened sense of smell for . . . you know,' said Peg, cocking a head in Oswin's direction.

The kobold turned to give him a highly affronted look, which lasted for much longer than was strictly necessary. Willow made no comment.

'We should go,' pressed Twist.

Oswin grumbled, **'Takin' fings from a kobold. No respect . . . I is a fearsome monster . . .'**

Twist stared at Oswin pointedly with those piercing eyes of hers. 'Are you quite finished?'

Oswin blinked and stopped

his grumbling at once, going to hide behind Willow's legs.

Willow thought she could do with learning that trick, especially at night when she was trying to sleep.

'Your bag should be ready when we come back,' Twist told the kobold. 'Come on.'

They followed her into the city as the sun began to set and the sky above turned pink and apricot. Outside, lamps fixed into the marble walls began to glow amber as they walked by, sensing them before they even approached.

They continued down a winding marble street, where they could see elves sitting outside cafés, drinking wine, while others leant against their balconies, talking and laughing. Many of them waved at Twist as she went by.

They passed bookshops where elves were reading in big comfy chairs, cups of tea balanced on their knees.

There was a large outdoor theatre where some elves were putting on a play, dressed up as strange woodland creatures. Beautiful music was being played by a Mementon – a creature with skin made of

wood, whose kind were known to be the best broom-makers in Starfell. This one was tall with russet-coloured hair and long nails, and he was playing what looked like a broom-guitar beneath the shade of a large marble archway.

It all seemed so alive to Willow, who'd grown up in a village where, unless it was a festival like Elth Night or harvest time, all outdoor activities faded as soon as the day did.

Twist took them to the heart of the city, where they entered a walled garden that smelt of roses and jasmine. The marble walls lit up as they entered, casting a soft hue that bathed them in pink light.

In the centre of the garden was a large fountain, featuring an elvish woman made of copper that had turned green over the years. Soft music played in the fountain, and the spray filtered down into a large pond covered in pink and white lily pads.

It was beautiful.

'The mural is here,' said Twist, leading them to the back of the garden.

The mural was massive, covering every inch of the enormous wall at the back, and it was extraordinary. Willow could only imagine the time and incredible skill something like this must have taken to create. It was a huge mosaic made up of small tiles in shades of rich turquoise, green, silver, pink and gold, though Willow noticed that many of the tiles were missing.

The mural depicted the elvish queen standing in a forest clearing. She was tall, with long midnight-black hair that had been arranged in a strange, intricate style that fell over her shoulder, all the way to her waist.

Her clothing was very different to what elves seemed to wear nowadays. The dress was beautiful, long and gathered, with loose, wide sleeves, and was tied with a sash at the waist. On her feet were simple leather shoes that were laced up her calves with ribbons. There were chips and cracks along the queen's arms, where tiles had fallen off.

All around her were hundreds of elves of all ages, staring up at her as she pointed in the distance with a spiralled staff. At the end of the staff was a half-circle shape, but they couldn't make out the rest as a cluster of marble tiles were missing.

'It's Queen Almefeira, pointing the way to the elves' new home,' whispered Twist. 'With the elf staff.'

'She sent them away?' asked Peg.

'Yes. Before Llandunia disappeared, the queen urged

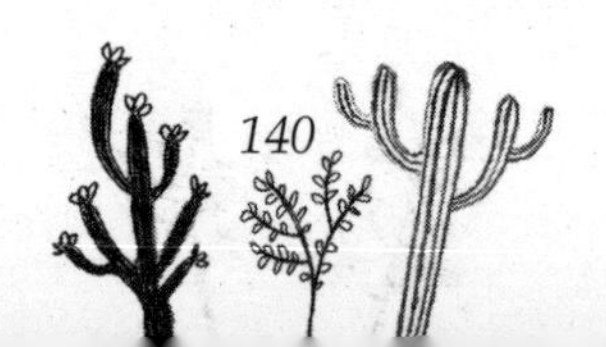

her people to leave and build a new city. And one of their first tasks when they were founding Lael was to create this mural . . . The work was carried out only by her family.'

'No servants or anything? That's kind of weird for royalty, isn't it?' asked Peg.

'It's because of the marble. Like I said before, the marble will choose you. While the city's walls and streets will remember us all, only the marble that chooses you will respond to you.'

'So . . . how has the mural responded to you?' asked Willow.

'Come, I'll show you,' said Twist.

She moved closer to the wall, held out her hands and touched the mosaic.

Like it had back in the elves' home, the marble started to glow beneath her fingers, and then the image began to shift, coming alive, like the emblems on the houses. But this was so much more than even that. This was a hidden story.

In the centre of the mural was a beautiful crystal city, surrounded by a shimmering lake. A red dragon flew over it, and the marble tiles changed from blue to pink to show the sun beginning to set. In the sky

were Starfell's two moons and, here and there, between missing marble tiles, was a smattering of stars.

Then suddenly the queen was alone in the forest clearing. She turned, and it was as if she were looking right at them, as if she were trying to show them something.

As she moved the spiralled staff, it was no longer obscured by the patch of missing tiles and they could see it clearly for the first time: at the end, a white orb was suspended by magic, and framed on each side by a half-moon shape. One was depicted in gold, the other in iron-grey. It was just like the spire on top of Howling House, Willow realised.

The queen then began to twist the gold half-moon towards her, and the crystal orb started to glow with a bright golden light. The queen then took the staff and pointed the golden light at a small fluffy hare that was hurrying past. The hare paused, and then golden wings suddenly appeared at its shoulders, and it started to fly.

'That's amazing!' cried Willow and Peg as the hare flitted here and there between missing marble tiles.

The queen adjusted the staff again, this time twisting the dark half-moon. With that, the crystal

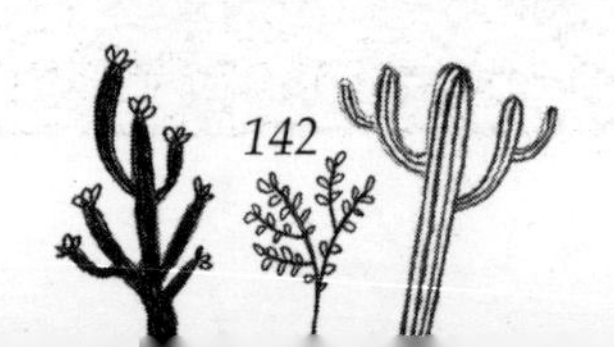

changed colour, becoming a deep black onyx. She pointed the staff once more at the flying hare. With a bolt of darkness, its golden wings disappeared and the hare fell to the ground. It suddenly appeared wasted and thin, like it was sick . . . like it had aged in an instant.

Then the mural changed back, becoming inanimate once more.

'That's the elf staff,' breathed Willow.

'Yes,' said Twist. 'Most elves know the legend – that once there was a great elvish queen with a powerful staff that could give the gift of magic. But I don't think any elves knew that it could take magic away too. I think that was kept a secret – because if that knowledge fell into the wrong hands . . . it could be the end of magical folk.

'Queen Almefeira hid the truth so that only her descendants would find out. But I think, as time passed by, it was sort of forgotten – perhaps a keeper of the secret died before she could pass it on to the next generation. We knew our family made the mural, but I don't think any of us really thought about whether it would respond to our touch. It was only when I watched a play recently about the history of Lael, and

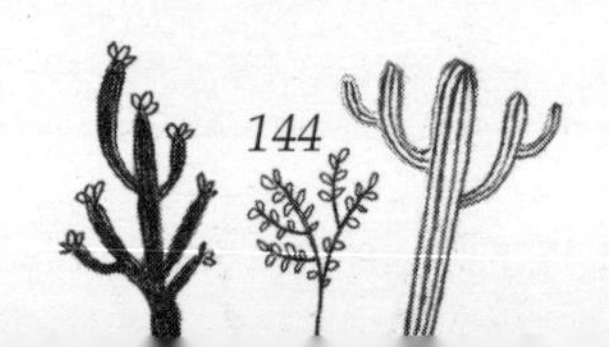

it showed the royal family creating the mural, that I began to wonder about the marble.

'It felt like a way to connect to the past – which seemed important because so many strange things have been happening that have odd links to history. The Brothers of Wol are growing more powerful and doing things they did years ago, like binding witches with manacles or creating more Forbidden areas to separate magical folk from the rest of the population . . . So I came here to explore, and I discovered this!'

Willow nodded. 'Yet somehow Silas has found out too,' she said. 'When I was in Netherfell, I learnt that he'd uncovered the secret method used by Wol in the Long War to strip people of their magic. I bet it was the elf staff.'

'It must've been,' agreed Twist.

Peg nodded. 'And he's stolen the scroll so he can use its message to find the lost kingdom. But if that does happen – and he gets the staff – will people . . . die?'

'Yes,' said Willow. 'This is bound to cause another war, and Silas will stop at nothing to win it. If he succeeds, magic will be ripped out of every corner of

Starfell and every person and creature . . .'

Peg's eyes grew wide with fear. 'And it looks as if it can be more dangerous than just losing an ability. Like that hare. He was fine when he was given magic, but when it was taken away . . . it was as if he aged, as if the queen took something else too.'

Willow paled. 'It was like part of his soul was taken.'

They stared at each other in horror.

'We can't let Silas get the staff,' said Peg.

They nodded, eyes wide.

It was now more important than ever to stop him.

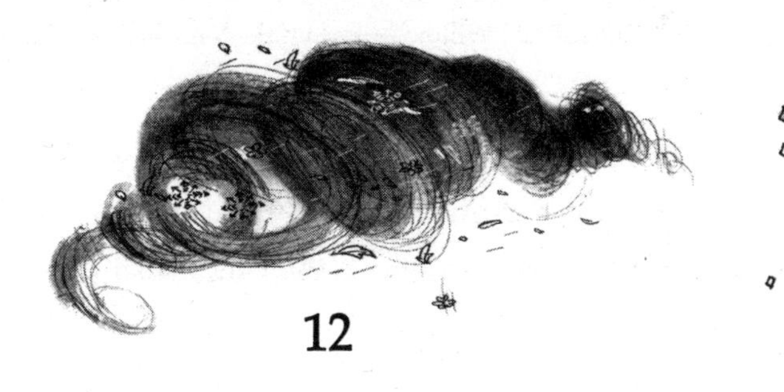

12

Written in the Stars

'Wait, Twist, didn't you say you thought the mural was trying to tell you something else, and you didn't know what?' said Peg.

'Yes,' said Twist. 'I can feel it through elfsense. I think it could be connected to the missing tiles. Maybe, if it was fully restored, it would tell us something more.'

Willow nodded. She'd been wondering the same thing. 'I'll try to find them,' she said. She closed her eyes and concentrated, then held her hand to the sky. A moment later, a dozen pieces of coloured tile rained down at their feet.

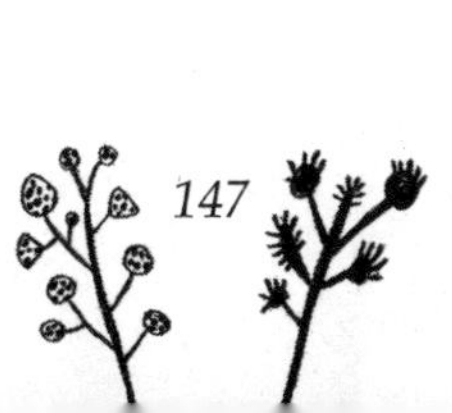

They stared at them for a moment. Peg scratched his head and said, 'I suppose we try to match the different coloured tiles to the picture in the mural – like a puzzle?'

Willow nodded. 'That makes sense.'

'This should go here,' said Twist, holding up a green tile and placing it in a missing section in the forest scene. There was a faint glow, like a guttering candle, and then the tile fell back off into her hands. 'Oh!' she cried. 'How can we make it stick?'

Oswin padded closer. **'Give it 'ere,'** he suggested.

The elf handed him the tile, a puzzled look on her face. He gave the back of the tile a lick, then passed it back with an air of nonchalance.

Twist reluctantly took it from him, pulling a face. 'Ugh. It's so sticky.'

'That wos the ideas,' said Oswin, rolling his eyes. **'Kobold spittles is a bit like glues.'**

Twist placed the tile in the empty space, and they watched in amazement as it fit like a glove, held firmly in place by Oswin's saliva. It began to glow, changing from green to faintly pink – the elfsense was working.

'Brilliant!' cried Twist.

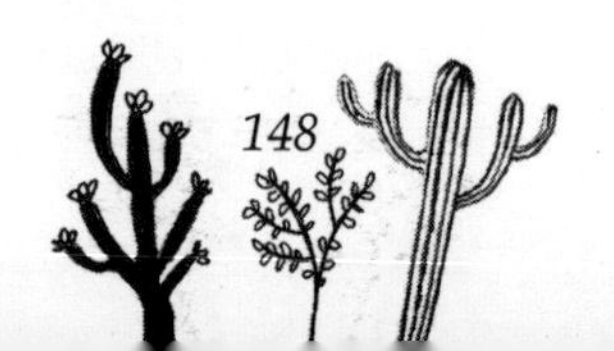

'I didn't know your . . . erm, saliva could do that,' said Willow, staring at the kobold in astonishment.

He looked at her in surprise. **'Why do you fink the Flossy Mistress always used ter tell me, "Get out of here, kobold, lickety-spit!"?'**

It was true. Granny Flossy had said that to him. A lot.

Willow, Twist and Peg shared a look that fortunately the kobold missed.

'Cos she wanted me ter seals up the cracks and fings in the walls, yew see?'

'O-*kay*,' said Willow, deciding not to let Oswin in on the fact that Granny Flossy had meant for him to leave the room pronto so she could brew her potions in peace – without him complaining that the room smelt funny or hiding behind furniture and warning Willow that things were likely to explode (which they were).

They got to work, colour-matching tiles. Oswin licked each one before it was put in place, and then they were left with just three for the very top of the mural.

'We'll have to climb on each other's shoulders, I think,' said Peg.

Twist nodded. 'I'll go at the bottom. I'm stronger than the pair of you.' They stared at her in surprise, and she said, 'Oh sorry – the direct thing, yes. Well,

it's true. To withstand storms and the like, elf bones are a bit like marble . . .' And then she stomped a foot down hard. For just a second, it looked like she was having a temper tantrum, but it turned out to be a display of strength, as she'd left behind a sizeable dent in the ground. 'See?'

'Wow!' said Peg. 'I mean, you don't look that strong.' Then he blushed. 'I mean . . . you just look like a normal, erm, girl.'

Twist shrugged. 'I know. Anyway, climb on,' she said, kneeling down so that Peg could clamber on to her shoulders. Then she held out a hand so that Willow could use it as a ledge to stand on top of Peg.

Swaying slightly on Peg's shoulders, her heart in her throat, Willow managed to place two tiles, but was still just a few inches too short to reach the top of the mural for the very last one. So Oswin scrambled up their pyramid to stick it in place, giving it an extra lick for good measure.

Twist placed her hands on the completed mural, which began to glow – just as Peg started to lose his balance and they all began to topple off . . .

'Skiron!' cried Twist. 'Catch them!'

And the wintry wind gusted itself round them and broke their fall, before releasing them gently on to the ground.

'Th-thanks,' said Willow, teeth chattering from the sudden cold. Then she looked up and gazed open-mouthed at the mural.

The colours had intensified and the scene looked sharper now, more focused. They all stared in astonishment.

Willow scanned it for any clues. 'Do you see anything new?'

Despite how much clearer the image had become, and the fact that the queen's hand and the staff were now filled in, it didn't seem to give them any information they didn't already have. They could see the dragon more clearly as it flew, along with the crystal city shimmering in the distance. Above it, the sky was fading from dusk to night.

'Not really – just more stars in the sky,' said Twist with a frown. 'And the dragon's long feathery body.'

Peg was the one to exclaim in shock. 'There is something else!'

'What?' asked Twist and Willow, turning to him in surprise.

'There! Can't you see it? That string of stars there.' He pointed and they looked, frowning. 'Have either of you seen that constellation before? It looks almost like a flying turtle.'

Twist, Willow and Oswin shook their heads and shared puzzled looks, not getting Peg's excitement.

'Well,' said Peg, 'many people still navigate by the stars – their position in the sky can let you know where you are and where to go. You can see different constellations from different parts of Starfell – for example, from Grinfog, you can see the old hag and the man who lost his shoe, as well as the big dinner party . . .' At their bemused looks, he explained, 'I'm really into astronomy, and I know all of the constellations of Starfell today –

but I don't recognise that one!'

He seemed thrilled about it, and Oswin muttered, **'Imagines getting exciterites cos yew don' know somefinks.'**

'It *is* exciting, though,' said Peg, staring up at the mural, eyes alight. 'The positions of stars can change over time, so this must be a constellation that existed a thousand years ago. If we can find out what that constellation is and where it could be seen from, we'd have a good chance of finding out where *the lost kingdom* was!'

Willow's mouth fell open. 'Peg, you're a genius! If we knew where it used to be, I *might* be able to summon it back – if it were safe . . .' She had visions of a city being split apart as the lost kingdom burst in somewhere it wouldn't fit . . .

Twist looked just as amazed. 'How on Starfell did you know that?'

'School can sometimes be useful,' Peg admitted. 'You know, when your teachers aren't trying to brainwash you or steal your magic.'

They all laughed.

'One thing I noticed is that the moons are close together in this mural, unlike today,' said Twist.

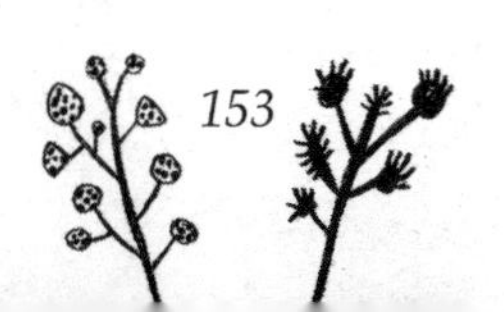

'Do you think that, when the kingdom vanished, it made them split apart?'

'Maybe,' said Peg. 'It's like what you were saying, Willow – about how magic can't just make things disappear and reappear without consequences. Maybe the position of the moons was one of them.'

'Maybe,' she agreed.

'Anyway, what we'll need are some really ancient star charts,' said Peg, but then he faltered. 'But those might be hard to find.'

To their surprise, Twist grinned. 'Here? Not on your elf! History keeps this city running. I know just where we need to go.' At their looks of confusion, she said, 'The Luminary. If anyone knows about stars and charts, it's the lumieres.'

'Oh nooo! Oh, me 'orrid aunt, do all roads lead to eel?' cried Oswin. **'Not 'em light-bending cumberworlds!'**

Something had changed.

A goose flew past, a second too late. The wind changed direction. The trees shifted their roots.

The witch looked behind her and saw, once again ... the ghost hare.

It always seemed to appear whenever she thought of going back.

A raven cried overhead, and she raised her hand to the sky. The bird began to fly towards her, one of its wings dark blue and made of what looked like smoke and shadow.

Then, before her eyes, the raven changed into the shape of a young boy.

'Moreg,' he greeted her.

The witch nodded at him. 'Greetings, Sprig.'

They stared at each other for some time. The renewed trust between them was fragile.

'I came looking for you.'

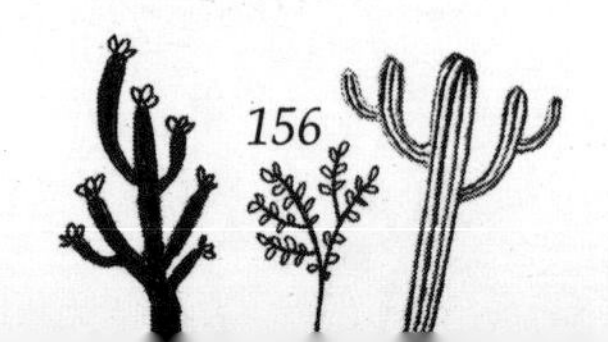

'Yes,' she said simply.

'Something is wrong. People are acting strangely . . . Willow is—' he began.

'Is stepping into something dangerous – I know.'

He looked surprised. 'I was going to say that Willow is the only one daring to go against the Enchancil. If she's in danger, aren't you going to go and help? No one's seen you for months.'

Moreg's face looked full of regret. 'Every time I take a step towards her, it changes . . .' She tried to explain. 'The course . . . falters.'

'So you're going to do nothing at all?'

'Sometimes that's what is required,' she replied, before walking away.

Sprig stared after her for some time, his dark eyes full of confusion.

There was a cry, and he was gone, flying once more against the darkening sky.

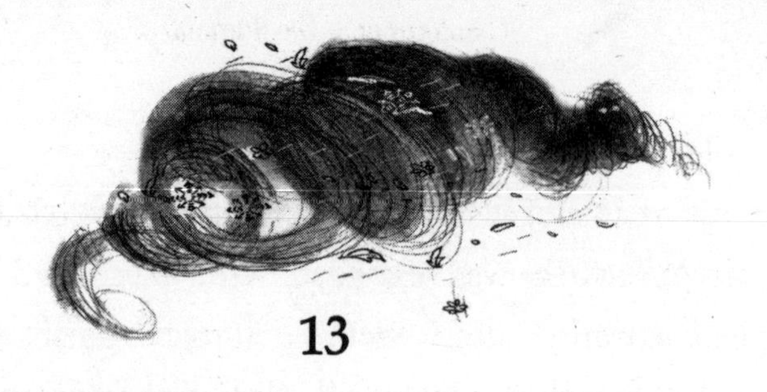

13

Gandolfo's Circus of Wonders

'We'll take a portal walk to the Luminary – it'll be quicker,' said Twist.

'A portal walk?' asked Peg. 'What's that?'

'I'll show you,' Twist said, and they followed her out of the walled garden to a busy square. Here neat lines of elves were queueing up. Ahead they could see signposts that read:

Each sign pointed towards a specific coloured lane.

'You want to keep to the white marble till we're

able to take our chosen lane and pop out at our destination,' Twist said, leading them up the marble street, which was crowded with elves and a few Mementons. 'There used to just be portal station points, but they got too crowded, so they made whole streets into portals. It helps with the flow of traffic,' she explained. Up ahead, they could see a thick ribbon of yellow alongside another of blue.

'Excuse me, we're in a hurry! The show is starting,' said a tall elvish couple in dazzling robes who were bustling past.

Peg jumped out of their way and on to a blue lane, just as Twist cried, 'Peg, no!'

He turned round to look at her in surprise, and then vanished into thin air.

'Oh no!' cried Willow.

'He's taken the portal walk to Gandolfo's Circus! Come on,' said Twist, dashing towards the blue lane. Willow followed. Before she could even ask any questions, there was a whooshing sensation and she felt herself being pulled away from the square. Seconds later, she was standing somewhere else entirely.

Ahead of her stood a giant red-and-white striped tent, and above it thousands of tiny multicoloured stars that formed the words GANDOLFO'S CIRCUS OF WONDERS lit up the sky. The atmosphere was electric and the crowds were enormous. She couldn't see Twist or Peg.

Oswin skittered up her leg and into her arms. **'Oh, me 'orrid aunt!'** he cried as people jostled past them, tickets in hand, ready to join a very long queue that snaked round the portal walk.

Willow's heart started to thud, and she let out a small scream when someone grabbed her elbow.

'It's only me,' said Twist. 'Sorry, someone thought it was a good idea to try pushing me out of the way.'

To Twist's left, Willow saw a tall elvish man who looked as if he'd put his clothes on backwards and his fingers into an electrical socket. He walked quickly past, not meeting Twist's eyes.

She, however, stared at him. 'Ashamed, eh? Yep – you should be for shoving over a little girl.' Then she looked at Willow and grinned. 'Not that anyone would call me that.'

Willow smiled. 'They wouldn't dare.'

Twist looked around. 'Have you seen Peg?' she asked.

'No,' said Willow, just as a large animal trumpeted behind them.

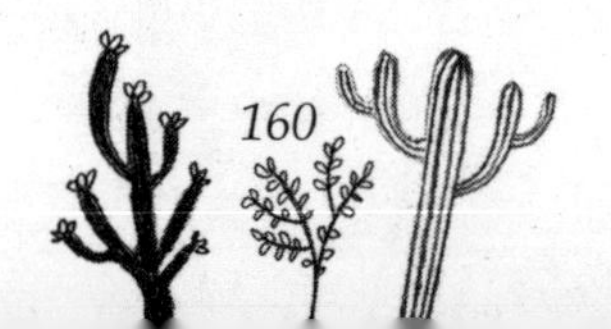

They turned to see an elephant topped by an acrobat. She was doing an impressive act on the animal's back as it slowly moved towards the enormous tent.

'Oh Wol,' breathed Twist. 'I should have explained better to Peg that the colourful lanes were portals to other places. I keep forgetting that he doesn't know much about magic! Come on.' She grabbed Willow's hand and elbowed her way out of the queue.

They moved through the crowds, calling Peg's name as they passed other circus performers, who were doing tricks to entertain the queueing crowds. There were card tricks, and jugglers, and a man who shifted into the shape of the person he was standing next to, making the customers laugh nervously as he did silly things while looking like them. There were winged monkeys who did a kind of aerial dance while screeching at each other, and a tall, beautiful, midnight-skinned woman, who had horns on either side of her head like a ram, was dancing with what looked like a ribbon of light.

It was incredible.

GANDOLFO'S CIRCUS
OF
WONDERS

There were stalls selling food, from mouth-watering sausages to sticky lemon cakes. There were bubbles of all shapes and sizes floating round a colourful stall, and someone called out, 'Sip a bubble, taste the wonder . . .'

'He could be anywhere! I've got a better idea. This way,' Willow said, pulling Twist to the back of a stall where someone was selling animals made from clouds.

'Lookin' cost you nuttin', but if you touchies, you paysies,' said an old woman, who was knitting bits of cloud into the shape of a winged monkey.

They nodded.

She looked at Oswin, then gave him a gummy smile. 'Eh, that's a funny-lookin' cat . . .'

The kobold glared at her. **'I is not a—'**

'Not now, Oswin. I need to focus,' said Willow, closing her eyes as the kobold continued to glare at the old woman. She just grinned back and, needles clicking, started to fashion a piece of cloud into a furry cat.

'What are you doing?' Twist asked Willow.

'Finding him the old-fashioned way,' said Willow, holding out her hand to the sky.

A moment later, Peg appeared in a heap on the

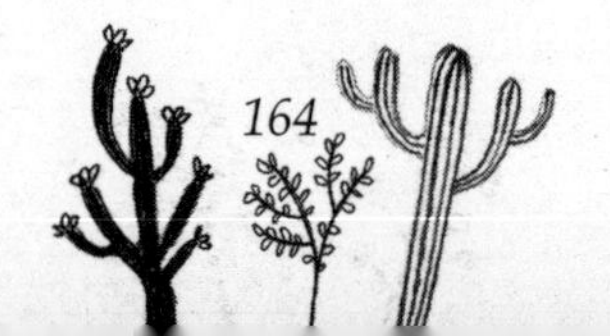

ground. He was covered in glitter and there was a sausage in his mouth – which landed in the dirt, to his dismay.

'Wha—?' he cried. 'I was just about to see the Crystal Peligraine!'

'Sorry,' said Willow, who assumed that was some kind of circus act. 'We were worried about you.'

Peg stood up, dusting himself off, and admitted, 'Well, it *was* a bit scary. One minute I was with you, the next I was here – at a circus!' His eyes were bright. 'Absolutely wild! Never seen so many strange things . . .'

'Never been ter the circus before?' asked the old woman. 'Need some tickets?' Magically, four red tickets appeared in the air above their heads.

'Sorry, we don't have time,' said Willow.

Peg looked a little disappointed, and the old woman said, 'Fer half a spurgle, you can have a memento of yer cat.'

'Go on then,' said Peg, handing over the money and taking a cloud balloon that looked just like Oswin, fur standing on end and everything.

The kobold turned a blood-orange colour in his rage, and the old woman looked at him and said,

'Word ter the wise, kobold: there's no shame in being who you is.'

Smoke curled off Oswin's ears as he began to hiss, **'But I is not . . .'**

'A cat, no, but are yeh gon' let that rule yer life forever? You looks like one. 'Tisn't a bad thing, is it? Mebbe you could use that to yer advantage someday. Think about it.'

Which was when Oswin exploded.

Luckily, no damage was done.

'Sorry,' said Willow, but the old woman just shrugged and carried on knitting.

'Advice is fer free. 'Sides, he probably needed to get it out of his system.'

Willow looked at Oswin after he'd calmed down. He did look better for his explosion.

'Let's get out of here,' said Twist.

Willow, Peg and Oswin followed her away from the crowds to the right portal walk, the yellow one, and they jumped on to it together.

After the excitement of the circus, it was a relief to be away from all the crowds, noise, sights and smells. This new part of the city was quiet. A tree-lined

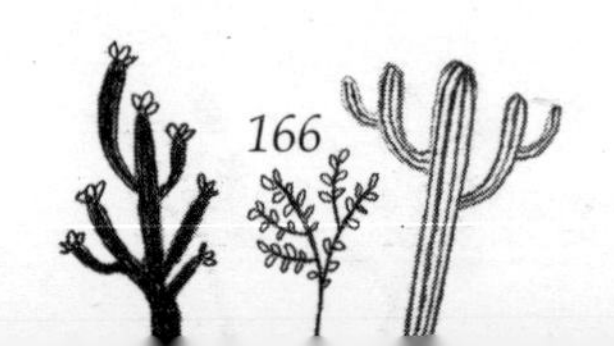

canal path led towards a large marble structure at the edge of the city that was shaped like a giant crescent moon and topped with a smattering of stars. The whole building glowed a faint greenish blue.

'It was built to reflect Jezelboob, the first moon,' explained Twist. At first, Willow and Peg didn't quite understand, until she pointed and said, 'Watch.'

A cloud passed over the real moon above, and the building changed colour too, becoming shadowed and grey.

'That's amazing,' said Peg. 'Is that what they do here? Study the stars and moons?'

'Yes, and all sources of light. The lumieres work with light energy, harnessing it and shaping it.'

Peg's mouth flew open. 'You can do that?'

'Me? No.' She held up her hands. 'You need lumiere blood to be able to handle light. They're elvish, but also something more.'

Willow thought of the Mementons, the broom-makers, who were part elf and part spirrot and distantly human. 'Are they like the Mementons?' she asked.

'A little. You'll see.'

'They is even worser,' whispered Oswin. **''Cept they don' eat humans.'**

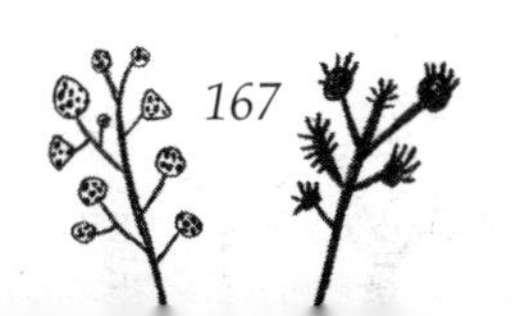

'Eat humans?' echoed Peg, letting go of his kobold-cloud in shock. It drifted away from his fingers towards the sky.

'Not for centuries,' reassured Willow.

'You've met lumieres before?' Twist asked Oswin.

'Yeh,' he groaned. 'Still got the scars.'

That doesn't exactly sound encouraging, thought Willow.

'The entrance is here,' explained Twist, leading them up a set of stairs at the side of the crescent-shaped building.

Unfortunately, a sign on the door said:

Helpfully, there was a bright display written in moonglow with the various moon phases and activities.

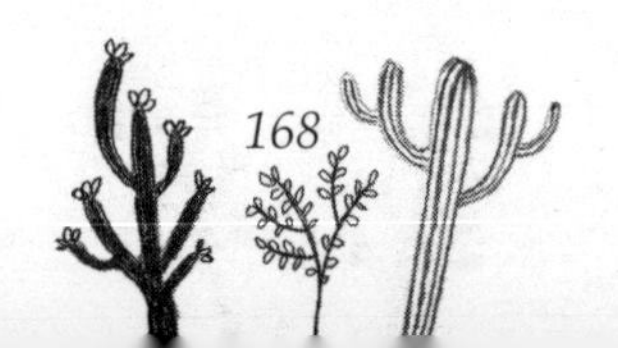

'Ah,' said Twist. 'Well, we could grab something to eat while we wait?'

At Twist's words, as if on cue, Oswin's and Peg's stomachs began to growl.

She grinned. 'Come on,' she said, and led them back down the steps.

Twist took them up a street that ran alongside a winding canal full of curved glass boats. Lights began to glow in lanterns set along the canal path as they walked by.

'The lumieres live in boats made of glass because they don't want to miss any changes to the stars or moons,' Twist explained as they passed one that was

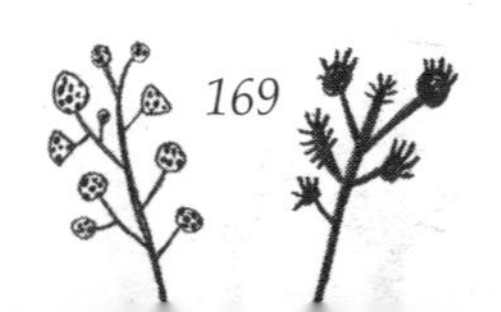

strung with strange wind-chime ornaments made of glass that tinkled in the breeze.

They could just see the outline of someone sitting on the roof of the boat, gazing up at the clouded sky above. The figure was playing a lively tune on a strange-looking brass instrument with strings that made a sound like a banjo.

Twist led the others to a small café with tables and chairs that overlooked the canal. The place was full of life, with elves chatting, laughing and eating together.

Willow, Twist, Peg and Oswin sat at a table outside, next to a large ash tree. Skiron started gusting through the air, and several of the customers began to complain of the cold, with one or two of them shooting Twist a pointed look – which she shot straight back.

'You know, Dot never gets dirty looks when her wind gets a bit overexcited,' she grumbled. 'Must be nice to tame a warm westerly wind.'

A waiter came to take their orders, and they enjoyed several courses – nut and leek soup, nettle pie and chocolate cake with fern nuts and blue cherries.

'I feels like a kobold again,' said Oswin, patting

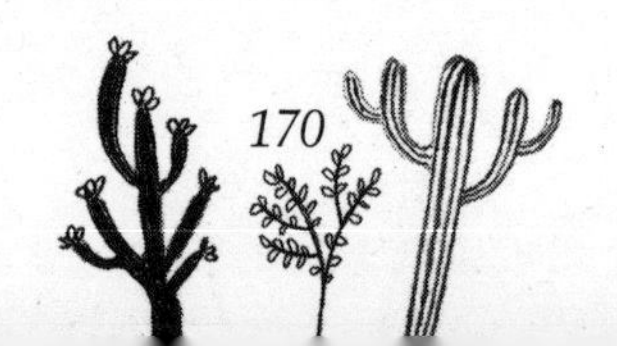

his tummy. **'All I 'ad to eats today was a sandwish wiff eel-liver paste and two gumbo apples, plus a loaf of bread, some cheese and twelve crackers.'**

'Which was both our lunches,' Willow pointed out. 'And all the food I'd taken to last us a few days.'

'Oh,' said Oswin. **'Sorry.'**

Willow sighed. 'That's okay,' she said. Missing food wasn't exactly new when your best friend was a kobold.

Though eel liver would never be top of her list, she felt a small pang, thinking of how her father had made the sandwiches himself. And how excited her parents had been at the thought of her going to school . . . She imagined them discovering the note in her room, telling them she wasn't going to be coming home until she figured out what was happening. She swallowed. They were not going to be impressed.

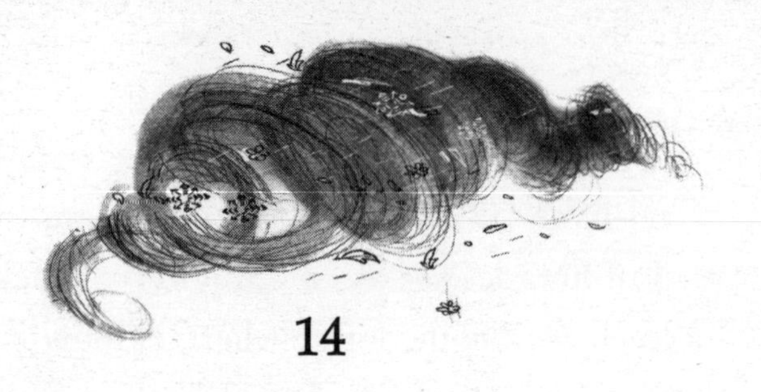

14

The Luminary

Clouds had passed over the moon, Jezelboob, by the time they made their way back to the crescent-shaped building. They could see a few people standing on the roof, adjusting strange bronze instruments.

Twist knocked at the door. There was the sound of light footsteps, and then it was opened by someone who looked a little like an elvish woman, but as the light from above hit her, she began to glow a faint pearly green colour, like the moon.

She must be a lumiere, thought Willow. She had long white hair and pointed elvish ears, and she seemed to be wearing a dress made of light that rippled as she walked. Her eyes were white, with tiny pinpricks for pupils.

'Can I help you?' she asked.

'We've come to find out if you have star charts from a thousand years ago,' said Peg.

The lumiere's eyes widened. 'And why is that?'

'Well, we've come across a constellation that we've never seen before.'

'We were just wondering if there was anyone we could talk to about that,' added Twist.

'You'll want archiving. Basement level.' The lumiere pointed to a staircase behind her, then grimaced. 'She's helpful. Just . . . try not to upset her. If you can.'

They followed a set of stairs down to the basement.

'What did she mean, "try not to upset her"?' Peg asked.

Oswin, however, was starting to whine. **'Oh noooo! Oh, me greedy aunt Osbertrude! Oh squifflesticks!'**

'What is it?' asked Willow, a little concerned.

But all Oswin said was, **'Oh, I wish I 'ad me bag! Oh nooo . . .'**

They found a small open door with a plaque that read:

In the corner of the little room, there was a desk cluttered with pens, scrolls and odd metal devices. Some reminded Willow a bit of her StoryPass.

Had she looked at the device, currently in her pocket, she would find it was now suggesting '*Cup of Tea?*'

A roaring fire was crackling in the grate, and everywhere there were piles and piles of scrolls, some on shelves that reached the ceiling, but others stacked on the floor in tottering piles.

'Oh, me greedy aunt!' cried Oswin, skittering out of Willow's arms and ducking behind her legs.

'Looks like there's no one here,' said Twist, looking around.

'Looks can be deceiving,' said a low voice coming, seemingly, from nowhere.

They whipped round. Willow's heart began to

hammer in her chest. There was no one there – just a small desk.

'Oh NOOOO! Oh, me greedy aunt Osbertrude. Oh, a kobold's curse upon yeh. I jes din't need this today.'

Willow frowned. Oswin usually only got this panicked when they were in the presence of powerful magic.

There was a screeching sound as a small sliding door in the desk began to open.

'What on Wol?' said Peg as a pair of large green eyes narrowed against the sudden brightness.

'Oh squifflesticks,' cried Oswin softly.

They couldn't see at first . . . and then the light hit the thing that stepped out from the desk. It was a small creature covered in green fur with several large white spots. In fact, if you didn't know better, you might even think it was a *cat.* Its ears had started to go a little orange as it peered at the space just behind Willow's legs and sniffed the air, a puzzled frown between its eyes.

Willow gasped. 'ANOTHER KOBOLD?'

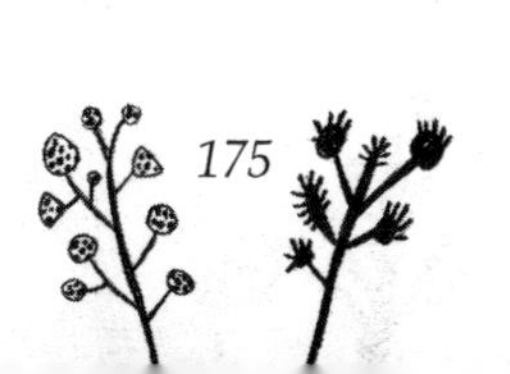

'Keep yer 'air on,' whispered Oswin.

The creature blinked. Then its eyes widened in shock as it breathed, 'Oswinifred?' Its posh, clipped voice took Willow completely by surprise.

Oswin's pumpkin-orange ears peeked out from behind her, followed by two large, rather glum-looking eyes.

''Lo,' said Oswin.

'Os-*winifred*?' whispered Willow.

'Not if yew values yer life,' hissed the kobold, and Willow bit back a laugh.

The other kobold looked delighted, her eyes filling with happy tears. 'It means so much to see family after all this time . . . I mean, even if it's, well . . . you.'

'You're family?' cried Willow.

'Tecknikly,' grumped Oswin. **'This is Osmeralda, me cousin.'**

Osmeralda dashed forward and squeezed him tightly. Then she wrinkled her nose and said, 'You know, Oswinifred, it wouldn't kill you to have a bath.'

Oswin turned a brighter shade of pumpkin as he muttered, **'I bave, every second Elth Nights . . .'**

Osmeralda rolled her eyes. 'Oh, Oswinifred, must we always go through this?'

‘Lewk, this is whys I don’ visits yew, as yew is always trying ter get me ter forgets that I is a kobold . . . Now, I’s gonna let the baving slew goes . . . But, for the last time, yew cumberworld, ’tis *Oswin*, no WINIFREDS necessary.’

Osmeralda sighed. ‘So touchy. Don’t tell me you’re still cross about that thing with Aunt Osbertrude.’

Oswin glared at her. **‘I don’ want ter talk about it.’**

‘But–’

‘I said I don’ want ter talk about it!’

Osmeralda sniffed. ‘Fine.’ Then she looked at Willow and Twist and sighed. ‘I apologise for the state of me. I’m usually better presented for company.’

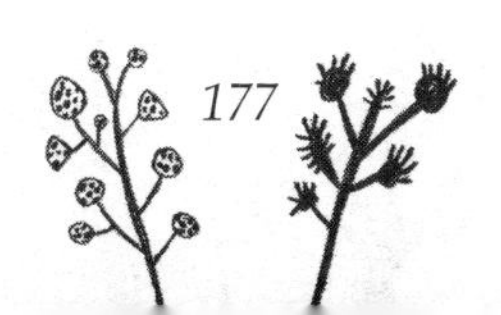

Willow was surprised at this, as Osmeralda seemed perfectly groomed – and even smelt a little of vanilla, something she didn't think was possible when it came to kobolds . . .

'So, to what do I owe the honour of your barging in?'

Willow and the others shared awkward looks.

'Well,' said Peg, 'it's about a constellation we saw.'

'Okay?' said Osmeralda.

'It's unlike any I've ever seen before – perhaps it's changed over the years.'

'That can happen.' Osmeralda nodded.

'We know *when* it was, if that helps,' added Twist.

'What do you mean?'

'The constellation we saw was in place around a thousand years ago,' she explained.

'How did you see it then?' asked Osmeralda, looking suspicious.

'Nones of yer business,' said Oswin.

'Now, look here, cousin. I am trying to be professional,' said Osmeralda with dignity.

'We saw it on a mural,' replied Twist.

The others looked at her, and she stared back. '*What?*' she mouthed.

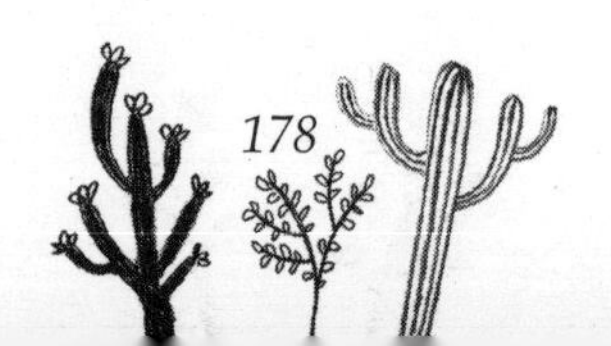

'A mural? You mean the one in the walled garden?' Osmeralda asked.

'Yes,' said Twist as the others groaned.

Willow felt it was perhaps not the best idea in the world to let on exactly why they needed these star charts. It would seem obvious that they were looking for the vanished kingdom – and this would surely lead to difficult questions. They didn't want to be stopped before they could get any further. Too much was at stake.

The trouble was, Willow suspected, that Twist had very little experience of lying. It must be really hard to do with elfsense.

'But you can't see any constellations there – too many tiles are missing,' Osmeralda pointed out.

'Willow found them,' said Twist, then she looked surprised as each of her new friends, including Oswin, put their heads in their hands.

Osmeralda looked curious. 'Willow . . . Moss?'

Willow looked up reluctantly. 'Er – yes.'

The other kobold frowned. 'The one from the paper?'

Willow winced. 'Yes – but look, I'm not actually delusional or anything . . .'

Osmeralda held up a green paw. 'Of course not.'

At their shocked expressions, she shrugged. 'My cousin and I might not see eye to eye, but if you were going around *telling lies* – well, he'd never be able to stand being near you. He'd explode every chance he got.'

'More than he already does?' asked Peg.

Osmeralda gave him what almost looked like a grin. 'Well, yes, just a bit.'

'Watch yerself,' muttered Oswin.

Osmeralda looked at them, and she suddenly seemed impressed. 'So that's what you're after – the vanished kingdom?'

They all blinked.

'You worked that out fast,' said Twist, and the others groaned.

'Twist, if you struggle to lie, can you just try not speaking in future?' said Peg.

Twist looked momentarily wrong-footed. 'Er – yes. I can try that.'

Peg sighed. 'Well, Twist has told you almost everything, so I may as well fill you in on the rest. We don't know where the kingdom has gone, of course . . . but, when I saw the old constellation, I thought

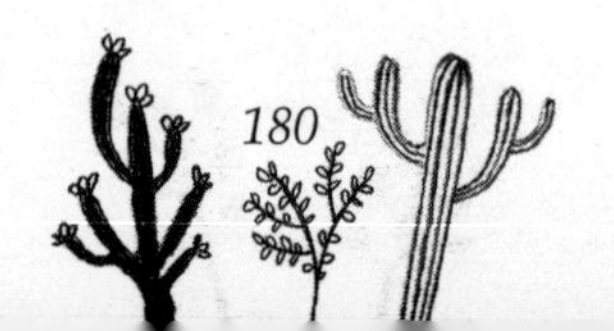

maybe we could figure out from that where it *was*.'

Osmeralda nodded. 'That makes sense.' Then she grinned. 'I daresay there's a few upstairs who would be willing to help with this. It's been eating them alive that some outsider might find Llandunia before they do – especially after the news that Queen Almefeira's scroll was stolen from Library.'

'Upstairs?' asked Willow.

'The lumieres,' she said, making her way to her desk. She popped a satchel over her shoulder, put on a pair of gloves and balanced some wire-rimmed glasses on the end of her nose. Then she crossed the room to one of the very tall shelves that went all the way to the ceiling and started to climb a steel ladder.

'The kingdom went missing during the Long War, so that's where we'll look. It makes sense that the stars would have changed since then – I mean, that's when the moons drifted apart too,' she said. 'If you can find your constellation in one of these, we can take it to Gibb. He'll probably have an idea.'

They watched as she wheeled the ladder between the shelves and stopped it with a paw. 'Mmmm. These look likely,' she called down as she pawed through old scrolls.

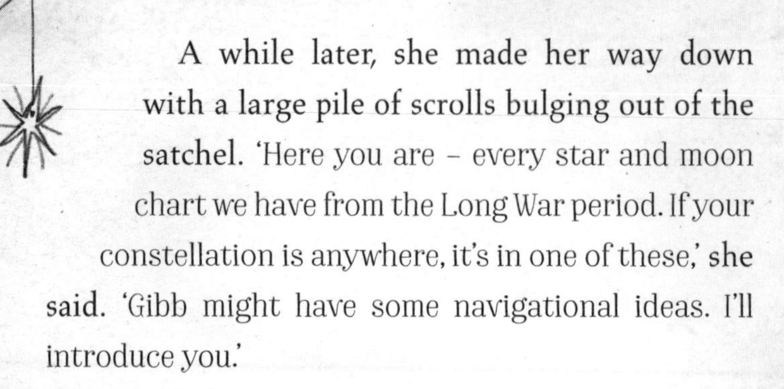

A while later, she made her way down with a large pile of scrolls bulging out of the satchel. 'Here you are – every star and moon chart we have from the Long War period. If your constellation is anywhere, it's in one of these,' she said. 'Gibb might have some navigational ideas. I'll introduce you.'

'And Gibb is?' asked Twist as the kobold led them back up the stairs that wound their way up the crescent-shaped building.

'He's one of the oldest lumieres and, er … is a bit of a fan of crackpot theories like yours.'

'Oi,' said Oswin.

'Just saying,' said Osmeralda. 'No offence meant.'

She led them all the way up to the roof of the building, past a group of lumieres who were hard at work, shaping light.

'What are they doing?' asked Peg.

'They're catching the moon's rays. See those big devices that look like telescopes?' she said, pointing at the large brass instruments they'd seen earlier. 'They catch moonbeams, and the lumieres channel the light. It helps to power the city and gets directed into the marble.'

'Wow,' said Willow.

'We also bring other things to life,' said an old lumiere, shuffling forward. He was tall, with a very long beard, and he had twinkling, almost mischievous eyes. Like the woman they'd met earlier, his skin seemed to glow a greenish colour like the moon, and he was wearing robes made of

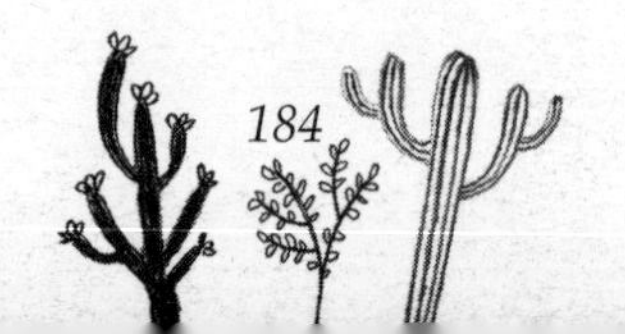

what looked like strands of light. At his shoulder, a small bird peered at them, then took flight across the starry night.

Willow blinked. Had that bird been made out of light?

'Gibbous Beam,' he said, holding out a finger. Twist pressed it with her own till a flurry of sparks danced between them, red and green, and Osmeralda introduced them all.

'Mmmm, interesting,' said Gibbous. 'I sense some kind of mystery . . . A plot is afoot.' He looked at Twist.

She grinned. 'You can't sense that!'

'Hee hee, nope,' he joked, but then tapped the side of his nose. 'The only reason anyone comes to find ol' Gibb is when they've got a mystery and they want to theorise . . .'

'That is a fact,' said Osmeralda, though she looked at the old lumiere fondly.

'Even a broken clock is right twice a day and all that,' he said. 'So, what can I help you with? I do sense some urgency – this is serious?' he asked.

They nodded.

To their surprise, he said, 'Has this got anything to do with that Enchancil waffle – and the nonsense about schools?'

'How did you know?' asked Willow.

Gibbous raised a pale brow. 'Eh . . . not exactly a stretch. Three kids, roughly the age range . . .'

'Oh,' said Twist, and she and the others grinned before returning to the serious subject at hand.

'Well,' began Willow, 'you're right that this is urgent.'

She and the others filled him in on what had happened at the school.

'Bless me heart!' Gibb cried, and in his anxiety he made several light creatures race towards him, including what looked like a mouse, a bird and a pony. He waved his hands and they scattered.

'So, them Brothers are at it again, trying to rid the world of magic?' he asked.

'Yes,' said Willow. 'That's why Silas is after the vanished kingdom—'

Gibb looked from Twist to Willow. 'Because something there is going to help him do just that?'

'How did you know?' cried Peg.

'Another one of his theories,' said Osmeralda.

Gibb nodded. 'During the Long War, magic started disappearing, right? Things got really bad. The Brothers of Wol were just about to succeed – and then suddenly Llandunia vanished, the queen disappeared and the war was over . . . The Brothers were defeated, and many years later, magic re-entered the world. Well, I always figured that whatever started to take away magic was somewhere in that kingdom, and without it, they failed . . .'

The others nodded, looking a bit amazed.

'So, you want to try finding it first – to stop them from doing it again?' he guessed.

Willow nodded. 'Well, yes.'

'You know, I like my theories more than just about anybody, but if no one has found that kingdom in a thousand years, I'm not sure how you will,' sighed Gibb.

Peg then explained about the mural and the strange

constellation he'd seen.

'That's why they've come to you. They want to see if they can find out where the kingdom was, using these star charts,' said Osmeralda, patting her satchel.

Gibb looked absolutely thrilled at this news. 'A missing constellation that might help us find Llandunia? Well now, that is a good puzzle to solve.' He danced on his feet, then hurried them over to a brass table and chairs.

'Let's have a look,' he said. He clicked his fingers and a small bright moon appeared above their heads, helping them to see better.

Osmeralda carefully unfolded the charts and they began to peer at them.

'Hmm, not that one . . . or that,' Peg said as Osmeralda unfolded chart after chart. 'What we saw looked a bit like a flying turtle.' He reached out a finger to trace the stars.

'Don't touch!' cried Osmeralda.

'Sorry.'

On the fourth one, he called out, 'Wait, that might be it! It did look a bit like this.' Peg pointed at a constellation.

'Ah yes, well, that's one we see in the west to this

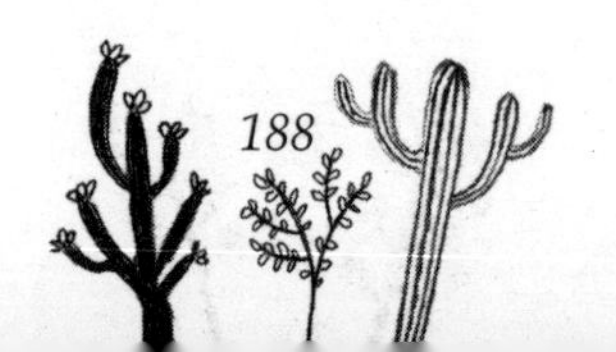

day – it's just changed a bit,' said Gibb.

Peg gasped. 'Oh! Yes, I see the tail now – am I right?'

Gibb beamed at him. 'Correct!' But, seeing the looks of confusion on the others' faces, he explained further by drawing the constellations in the air for them, using spots of light. 'You see, back when Llandunia was around, the stars were a bit different . . . like this.' He pointed at the flying turtle shape. 'But what if it's something you already know . . . just rearranged a little?'

Then he began to move the dots of light, spreading the two moons further apart and lengthening the constellation's 'body' so that it looked less like a flying turtle and more like a dragon.

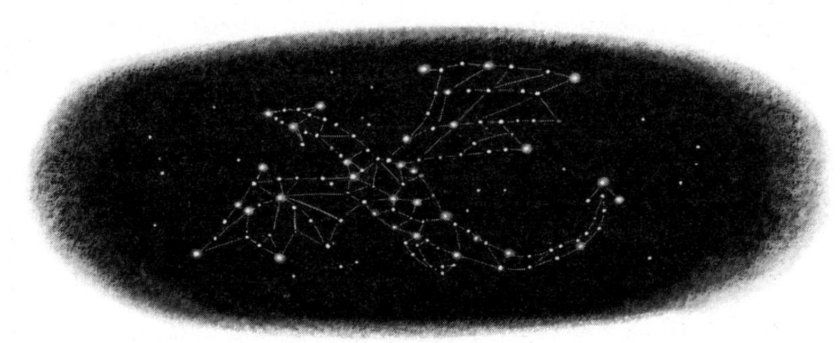

'It's the old winged dragon!' confirmed Peg. 'You can only see it from the west of Starfell!'

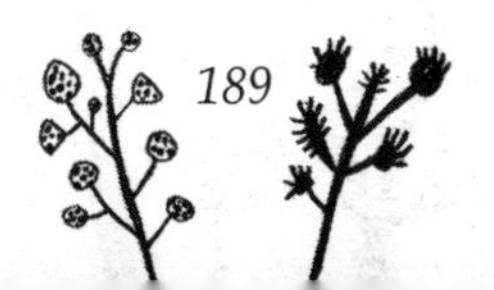

'Oh!' cried Willow, who had at least heard of that before. 'Could we chart where the kingdom was based on this?'

Gibb stroked his beard in thought. 'You'd need to cross-reference with quite a precise image of the stars over Llandunia in order to be accurate,' he said.

Peg shook his head, looking disappointed. 'The mural was just a loose representation.'

'How can you be sure?' Twist asked, surprised.

'Well,' explained Peg, 'look at how Gibb has drawn the moons. It's perfectly to scale. But in the mural, they were almost the size of the dragon. If that was off, so much more could be too.'

'Oh,' said Willow.

Gibb nodded. 'Very wise. One small mistake and you could find yourself in the wrong city or even country.'

Willow swallowed. This meant that they still didn't know where the vanished kingdom was. There were so many different western regions of Starfell – the Mists of Mitlaire, the mountains of Nach, Troll Country, Dwarf Territory . . .

'Funny you should mention a dragon,' said Gibb, interrupting her thoughts. 'Of course, there'd be no

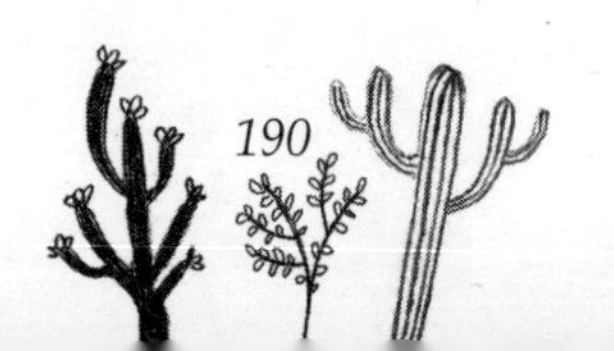

human or elf alive today who'd remember where Llandunia was, but . . .' He cocked his head towards the winged dragon constellation in the air before him. 'I've always thought that they'd probably have an idea. I mean, very few people have ever spoken to a dragon, but if anyone would know, it'd be them.'

Willow gasped. Of course! She had never thought of that before! 'Oh! Thank you, Gibb!'

'You're welcome,' he said, then laughed. 'I suppose! But good luck finding one . . . I've been alive over a thousand cycles and I've never even come close.'

'Hang on. What do you mean?' asked Peg.

'He means we need to talk to a dragon,' said Twist. 'And they're pretty impossible to find.'

Willow grinned, the dragon constellation shining in her eyes. 'It's hard, but not impossible. You just need to know where to look.'

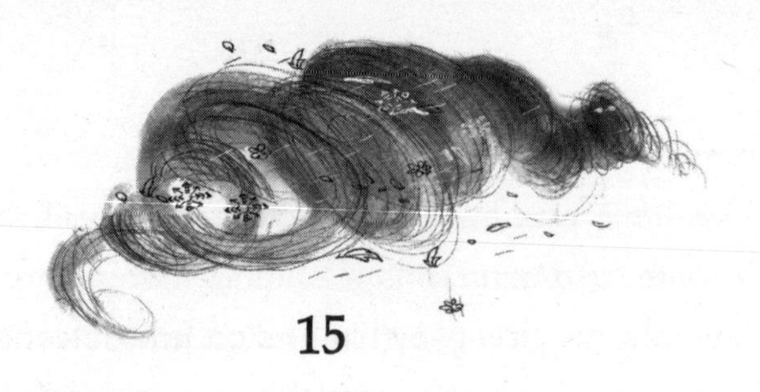

15

Broom and Breakfast

'You mean to tell me you know how to find a dragon?' cried Peg.

'Yes,' said Willow, and she explained about her friend Feathering the cloud dragon, and how, on their first adventure together, she had returned Feathering to his mate, Thundera, and got to meet their baby dragon, Floss.

'That's incredible,' said Twist, but she was stifling a yawn. It was well past midnight and it had been a long day. 'Gibb, Osmeralda, thank you so much for your help. I think the rest of us should go back to my house, get some sleep and head out first thing in the morning,' she said.

In Willow's arms, Oswin let out a snore. 'I think that's a good idea,' she said. Part of her wanted to just keep going, to try to find the kingdom before Silas

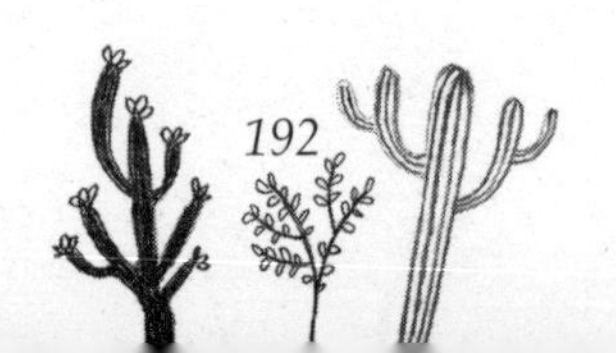

did, but she was dead on her feet.

With a last goodbye to Gibb and Osmeralda, they left the Luminary and took a portal walk back to the centre of the city. They trudged on leaden feet back to Twist's marble house, and Willow was grateful when the doors sprang open.

'This way,' said Twist. 'You can sleep in my aunts' rooms.'

Peg gratefully stopped at an autumn-coloured door, and Twist led Willow to a green one. Inside it was still warm and fragrant, like Dot's floral spring breeze.

They said goodnight, and Willow climbed wearily into bed, surprised to find that the sheets had already been turned down and a pair of fluffy socks was waiting for her on the pillow. She grinned. There was certainly a lot to be said for living in a sentient house.

There was a faint knock on the door, and something crept inside the room. Willow turned to find Scratch scurrying towards her on its long chicken legs. It was carrying her hairy green carpetbag on top, which it placed gently on the floor. It looked fluffy and clean.

'Thank you, Scratch,' she said.

The table gave a kind of bobbing nod, then scurried back out, closing the door behind it.

*

In the morning, Scratch brought Willow tea and chocolate ginger biscuits, and Oswin harrumphed as he examined the green carpetbag.

'Smells funny,' he moaned, taking things out and inspecting them – the troll whistle, a change of clothing for Willow and Oswin's nest blanket. The latter was pretty horrid, to be honest, as it was made up of all kinds of smelly junk. Or it used to be. Oswin sniffed a tin can and pulled a face.

'That's called clean,' Willow pointed out.

'Yeh, don' like that,' Oswin said. Then he reluctantly repacked everything and climbed in, and despite his grumbles, she heard a low sigh of satisfaction. There was a rattle from the blanket's array of cans and bottle caps as he pulled it over his head.

Willow shook her head, hiding a grin, as she picked up the bag and went to find the others.

She found Twist and Peg sitting in the kitchen, eating breakfast. It was cold, the air frosty and bright.

'Scrambled eggs all right?' asked Twist, lifting a spatula in greeting.

'Perfect.'

'Skiron, no! Come on, outside! Just once in my life, I'd like to have some warm food,' she moaned as the swirling, icy wind circled round her feet. '*Selia*,' she said, and it hurried outside. The air turned considerably warmer.

As Willow took a seat at the marble table, Scratch rushed forward to help her pull out an iron chair.

'I think I might have lost my heart to Scratch a bit,' Willow said, looking at the table fondly.

'Speak fer yerself,' muttered Oswin from the carpetbag. **'Smells in 'ere.'**

'Did you also get warm milk last night and an orange this morning?' asked Peg, pausing between mouthfuls of egg.

'No – I got biscuits, though, and warm socks,' said Willow.

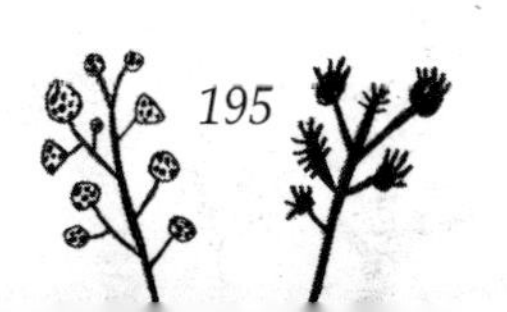

'It's the house,' explained Twist. 'It knows what you like.'

'That's wild,' said Peg. 'And it explains why it brought me this.' He held up a piece of paper and a pen. 'It knew somehow that I was feeling guilty about not going home. I should have sent my mother a letter earlier.'

Willow felt a stab of guilt. 'Sorry, Peg. I didn't even think . . .'

'Me neither,' Twist said.

'It's not your fault. Your aunts offered to take me home.'

'We still can, if you like,' said Twist.

'No, it's fine. If the house or Scratch can post this for me, though, that would be good . . . I still think it's important that someone non-magical understands what's been happening.'

They nodded.

'Besides,' he grinned, looking at them, 'it's been kind of fun . . . apart from travelling by tornado.'

They all laughed.

After breakfast, they headed outside.

'If you don't mind, Twist,' Willow said, thinking of

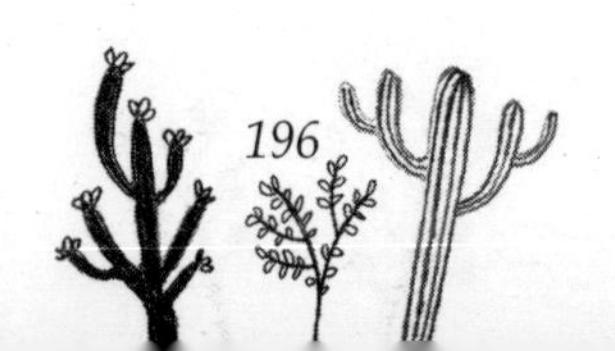

Peg's earlier comment, 'Peg, Oswin and I will travel by broom.'

Twist's mouth curved into a smile. 'Suit yourself.'

'I never fought I'd look forwards ter travellin' by this fing,' said Oswin, who looked greatly relieved.

And they set off on Whisper, flying north-east towards the Cloud Mountains. They passed over the colourful stalls of the Midnight Market, which were all closed, their proprietors waiting for the cover of darkness to sell their dodgier wares.

They flew over Radditch, the home of the Mementons who made brooms like Willow's. Willow pointed them out to Peg.

'Wow, that's incredible!' said Peg as they flew over a group of young broom-makers who were sorting twigs into piles while others were testing the new brooms. One flew pretty close, on what looked like a strange, new broom with colourful leaves at the end. The broom-maker had russet-coloured hair to match and waved at them before circling back to the forest below.

As they neared the city of Beady Hill, they spied some Brothers of Wol and a few soldiers on the ramparts, armed with flaming arrows.

'We can't fly over!' Willow shouted at Twist, who was hovering with Skiron close by. Willow had attempted to fly over this city once before with Moreg, but as it had Forbidden status, it was unlawful for magical people to enter or fly over. She and Moreg had faced a lot of trouble over it.

'Follow me,' said Willow, and they changed

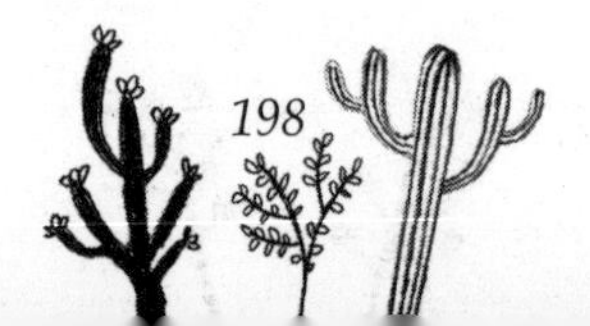

direction slightly, heading towards the long, winding Knotweed River, where delicate purple flowers shaped like bells grew and played their soft, haunting music.

'Don't listen to the music,' Willow told Peg. 'It'll lure you into the water – and there are all sorts of dangerous creatures in there.'

'Yup,' said Oswin, popping his head out of the

carpetbag. **'Merpeoples who likes ter snatch up kits likes yew. See, they has troubles having their own babies – 'tis hard cos they is all electeric.'**

Peg's eyes widened.

'The only fing they is afraid of is cats cos there is somefink about a cat that makes 'em lose power . . . When they founds out I *wasn't* actuallys a cat, a mer-king tried ter marry me off ter his daughter so he could make another tribes fink they was so powerfuls not even a cat could bovver 'em. Not that I is one, as you know,' he added fiercely.

Peg nodded quickly, sharing a look with Willow, who was a little surprised at the story too.

'Though ter be fair, I probably should 'ave told 'em I was . . . might have saved me a few scars,' continued Oswin, showing the boy three faint marks on his rear, which were right next to two recent ones from Twist's aunt, Tuppence.

Willow and Peg fought the urge not to laugh.

Peg shook his head in amazement. 'Did you know that about him?' he asked Willow.

'No, I'm always finding out something new,' Willow said, grinning, her eyes alight. Oswin wasn't

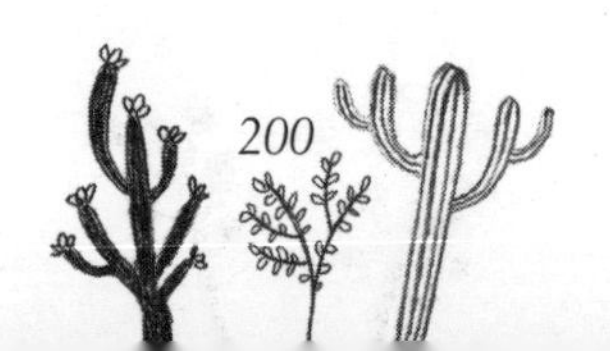

exactly talkative, but she did like hearing his stories.

Willow aimed Whisper up higher, away from the soft, enticing music of the Knotweed, and they followed the course of the waterway as the morning turned to afternoon. Birds kept pace with them, including a flock of pink-winged geese.

'I've never seen them that colour before!' cried Peg.

'Must be because we're so close to the forest of Wisperia,' said Willow, who filled Peg in on all the strange and beautiful creatures that lived in that magical place.

As they flew on, above the long green river, Willow couldn't help thinking of her friend, the sailor-wizard, Holloway, who had helped her cross into Netherfell. It had been some time since she'd seen him last. She wondered if he was involved with the wizards who'd been forced out of their homes in Beady Hill's Ditchwater district and were trying to take back their land . . .

They stopped for a quick lunch from one of the moored boats along the river. It was a long, narrow vessel that was serving fish soup with fresh crusty bread, which they ate in wooden bowls on the riverbank before continuing on their way.

They flew over the vast, colourful forest of Wisperia, and finally towards the floating Cloud Mountains, where they entered a mist so thick it was hard to see even a few feet in front of them.

'Oh nooo! Oh, me eyeballs!' cried Oswin.

Willow was struggling to steer Whisper.

'I c-can't believe we're going to meet dragons,' whispered Peg.

'I heard that they, um, eat people?' said Twist, who was swirling with Skiron nearby.

'Not any more! That's what Feathering said anyway.'

Peg looked amazed.

'I think he said something about going off the taste of them a few years ago . . .'

There was a loud gulp.

Willow grinned. 'I think he was joking.'

With her free hand, she dug in her pocket for the StoryPass. The needle spun round and round.

'That's strange,' she whispered. 'It's like it can't make up its mind.'

'H-how will we find the dragons?' Peg asked as Twist followed behind them, whirling in the wind.

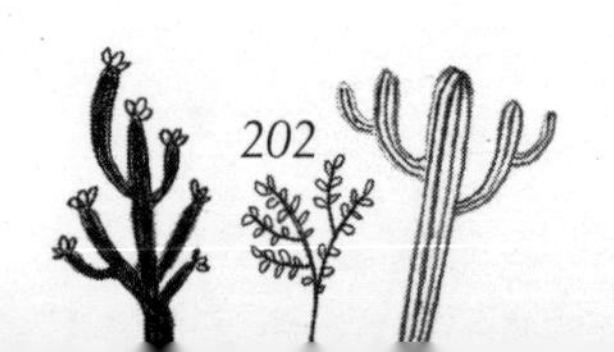

The needle in Willow's hand suddenly pointed to *'There be Dragons'*.

'Like this!' she said.

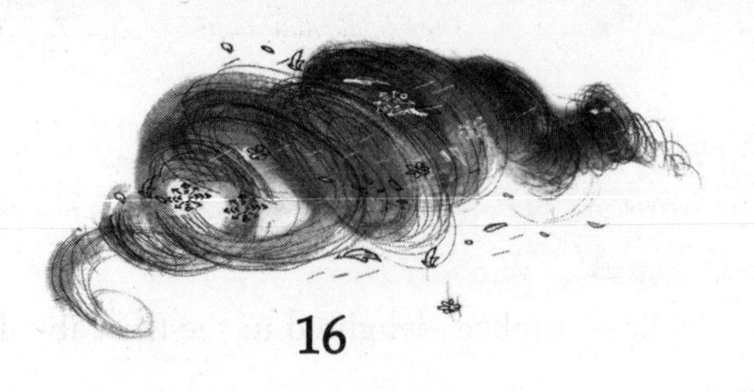

16

The Cloud Mountains

At that moment, a large blue shape emerged from the clouds above, followed by a red one and a smaller blue one.

'Feathering!' Willow called, waving.

'Hello, Willow! Oswin?' This was followed by laughter that sounded like a wind chime. 'And who is that with you, flying by tornado?'

'That's Twist.'

'Ah, elvish magic – haven't seen it in years!' called Feathering. 'Follow us. We'll lead you to a clear landing path.'

Willow and Twist followed the large blue shape ahead of them through the clouds. From behind them, a little voice called out excitedly, 'WI-WOW?'

Willow looked behind, then grinned. It was the baby dragon, Floss, who ambled through the sky like

a puppy, bouncing between the clouds.

'Look at me! Wheeee!' he said, doing a sort of somersault.

Willow laughed, delighted to see the baby dragon again.

'I can fly really high now!'

'That's wonderful, Floss!' called Willow.

She was amazed at how much he'd grown. He was about the size of a travelling wagon now.

'Follow us,' called his mother, Thundera, skimming through a bank of clouds towards the floating mountains. Her sleek feathers glistened in the sky like rubies.

Feathering landed first, the ground shaking with the force.

Willow and Twist circled above in the tailwind, while Thundera and Floss followed, landing with a running stop.

Willow introduced Twist and Peg to the dragons. Floss seemed very interested in the windswept girl. 'Your hair is funny,' he said.

'Floss!' Thundera scolded. Looking at the elvish girl, she added, 'Sorry.'

'But I like it,' whined Floss. 'How does it all stay up like that?'

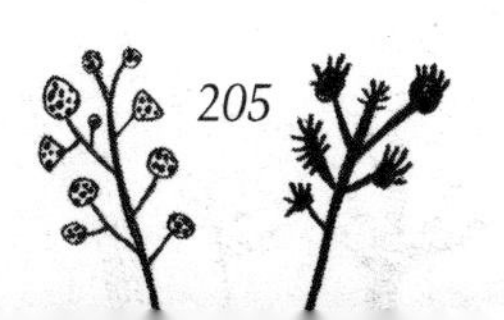

Twist grinned. 'The wind.'

As if in answer, Skiron spun round them, freezing the air till there were icicles at the ends of Floss's eyelashes. 'Brrr,' he said, shaking them off.

'It's good to see you, dear friend,' said Feathering, and Willow rushed forward to stroke his feathered face.

'You too.'

'We were so worried about you,' said Thundera.

'Me?' said Willow.

Feathering nodded. 'We flew over the Dark Woods and Grinfog yesterday to see if we could find you. On our flight paths, we have seen the Brothers of Wol rounding up children.'

Willow and the others gasped.

'We saw them marching long lines of children towards the fortress of Wolkana. It didn't look as if the young ones were behaving normally . . . There was no light in their eyes – and no one reacted to seeing a dragon,' said Feathering.

This was strange, as most people panicked at the sight of one dragon – so naturally, pandemonium would have ensued over seeing *three.*

'They is usin' Gerful chalk,' explained Oswin, peeking out from the top of the hairy carpetbag.

The irises in Feathering's eyes whirled in anger. 'That is immoral! It's been illegal for centuries!'

Willow nodded. 'It hasn't stopped them, though,' and she filled the dragons in on what had happened at the schools.

Peg shook his head. 'It looks like they're moving

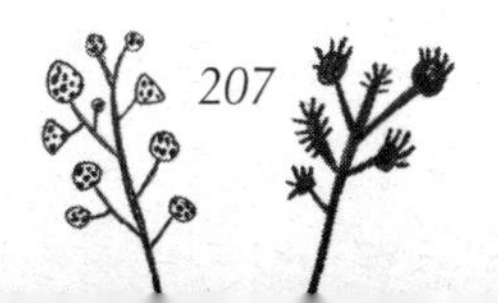

even quicker now, though. Cuttlefish, our teacher, implied that they were focusing on brainwashing kids about magic being unnatural. It sounded as if it would be some time before the children were taken anywhere . . .'

'I think it's because of my aunts,' said Twist. 'If they've assembled some people to spread the word and go after the Brothers, it might mean that the Brothers had to move their plans forward as a result.'

'Oh gosh, you're probably right,' said Peg.

Willow closed her eyes in horror. It was a horrible thought. 'We *have* to find the kingdom before Silas does,' she said. 'Before he's able to steal all their magic.'

'What do you mean?' asked Feathering. 'What kingdom?'

'The vanished elvish kingdom of Llandunia,' said Willow, who explained about the scroll, the staff – and the secret they'd discovered about what it could do.

'So that's what he's after – the elf staff,' said Feathering.

Twist looked at him in surprise. 'You know of it?'

'Oh yes, of course. I was just a hatchling, but I was around when the kingdom vanished . . . And even

back then no one really knew what happened. There one day – gone the next.'

'That's what we came to ask about!' cried Willow. 'To see if you remembered it.'

'Oh yes, it was a beauty – a great crystal city, as tall as the sky, with streets of marble and gold winking in the twilight. The crystal would catch the light, turning pink and purple, and the queen's warrior, Vermora, could always be seen circling the sky after the hunt. Fearsome, she was, with acid breath and talons of pure diamond. She was the last of the fire dragons, even then.'

Willow, Peg and Twist gasped.

'The queen owned a dragon?' Twist asked.

Feathering looked at her, and the elf had the grace to blush. 'I mean, she had a dragon companion?'

'Yes, she did.'

'But do you know where it was – the kingdom?' Willow pressed. 'We only know it was somewhere in the west. I feel like if I can find out where it *was*, then I could maybe try to bring it back . . . so long as I knew I wouldn't be harming anyone.'

He nodded. 'That makes sense. I could tell you roughly what I remember as a hatchling, but I think

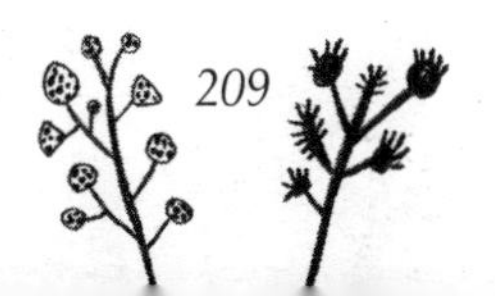

there are other creatures that would have a better idea. They'd be able to tell you exactly where it used to be, as they would remember it in their bones.'

'Who?' asked Willow.

'The rock dragons.'

Thundera sighed. 'Oh, Feathering, anyone but them.'

He nodded. 'They're difficult beasts. I'm not sure they'll agree to help, but there's always a chance. It will require a sacrifice,' said Feathering.

Peg and Oswin started wailing at the same time.

'**Oh no! Oh, me greedy aunt!**' cried Oswin.

'Oh why, oh why didn't I say I wanted to go home?'

Feathering made a sound like tinkly wind-chime laughter. 'Not that kind of a sacrifice. A trade – rock dragons will only help if you give them something in return. They don't relish coming out in the light.'

Willow wasn't the only one who sighed in relief. 'What should we give them?' she asked.

'Food?' suggested Twist.

'No, nothing like that, alas. It'll be something like your memories from when you were born or a promise to name your first child after them . . . and good luck with that. Their names are impossible . . .'

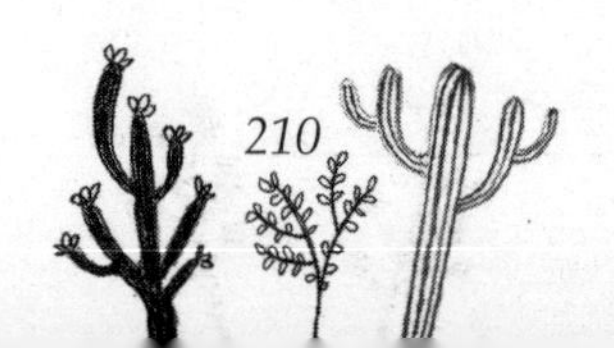

Willow, Twist and Peg shared looks of horror.

'I'm sure we'll manage, though. I'll help negotiate. Get on and I'll take you to them,' said Feathering.

Willow hesitated for a moment. Something else, something horrible, had occurred to her just then – worse even than the idea of giving up her memories to a fearsome rock dragon.

'Feathering, when you saw children being taken . . . was it still just those under the age of thirteen?' she asked.

Feathering frowned as he thought back. 'Oh . . . I don't know. Thundera?'

'Seemed a mix to me – younger and older,' said Thundera.

'Oh no!' said Twist. 'So they could have taken all the children, regardless of their ages?'

'I think so,' said Thundera.

Willow's stomach sank to her toes. 'My sisters!' she gasped.

'We can get them back. We'll help you,' said Thundera.

'Th-thank you,' said Willow.

'You go with Feathering. Floss and I will find your sisters and try to stop the Brothers,' said Thundera.

'We'll search for Essential and Sprig too.'

'Oh! Thank you,' breathed Willow, feeling a pang of worry for her friends.

Thundera nodded. 'We'll see you soon,' she said, and together she and Floss took to the sky.

'Be careful!' Feathering shouted after them.

'Always,' came Thundera's response.

'Bye, Wi-wow and fwends!' called Floss.

Willow waved, her heart torn as she thought of her sisters, but she had to carry on – she needed to find Llandunia. She needed to stop Silas before it was too late.

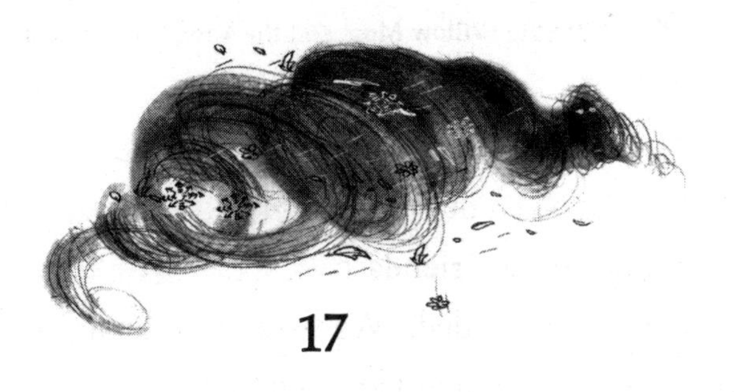

17

Rock Dragons

Willow and Peg climbed on Feathering's back. Willow used her scarf to strap her broomstick to her back.

Peg was shaking. 'Are you sure this is safe?' he gulped.

Oswin peeked his head out of his bag and muttered, **'Ridin' a cloud dragon, or goin' off in search of rock dragons?'**

'Uh . . . both,' said Peg nervously.

'Travellin' by dragons is better than that,' Oswin said, cocking his head in the direction of Twist, who had chosen to follow by tornado.

Peg swallowed. 'Yes. Anything's better than that.'

'Well, I am glad to see you've started to succumb to my charms, Oswin,' said Feathering with his tinkly wind-chime chuckle.

'As for the rock dragons,' said Willow, 'I don't see that we have a choice – we need to find Llandunia.'

'They live on the last of the Cloud Mountains,' Feathering explained, and with his massive wings, they flew there much faster than by broom. Even super-fast Whisper was no match for the cloud dragon.

Feathering landed on a rocky outcrop. It was less misty out here and barren. Then he made a strange shrieking sound that caused all the hairs on the back of Willow's neck to stand on end.

'It's the dragon call,' he explained. 'We use it when we are in need.'

'And they'll respond?' asked Willow, swallowing.

Feathering shrugged a massive blue shoulder, the iris in his eye spinning as he searched the ground. 'It's possible, though rock dragons follow their own rules.'

Twist whirled down shortly afterwards, patting her hair into place. Then she looked around with a frown. 'Where do you suppose the rock dragons are?' she asked.

A deep voice, like the earth cracking open during a drought, rumbled, 'We are everywhere and nowhere all at once. From the dirt to the pebbles to the stones,

we are beneath and all around you.'

'Oh!' cried Willow and Peg, who held on to each other as the ground beneath their feet started to shift and shake.

Small stones began to scatter, and rocks and boulders rolled, gathering before their eyes to form into a giant stone dragon. There was a hissing noise as its nostrils flared, and wind gusted in and out of them. Above its huge snout, the rock dragon revealed a pair of glowing lichen eyes. Its mouth opened into a yawning chasm, and Willow couldn't suppress a shudder. Should someone happen to slip and fall inside it, there might be no return.

Behind the large dragon, several other rock dragons began to form from the scattered stones.

Willow's heart began to hammer in fear.

'Oh WOL!' cried Peg, just as Oswin muttered, **'Oh no,'** very quietly.

'What is it that you want from us?' asked the rock dragon.

Feathering began to explain why they were there. 'To see your memories of what happened to the vanished kingdom of Llandunia – so that we can find it once more.'

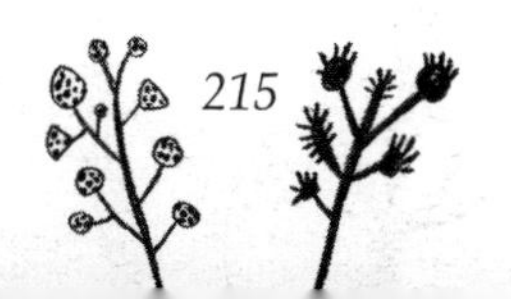

The rock dragon sniffed the air. 'And why would we tell you?'

'Because,' Willow pleaded, 'we need to know what happened. Someone is trying to find the kingdom, someone who wants to steal magic from Starfell. I – we – want to stop them.'

At the dragons' sudden outrage, there was the rumbling sound of rocks rearranging themselves. 'We have sensed this!' hissed the main rock dragon. 'Something is coming!'

Feathering nodded. 'There will be another war – unless we act soon.'

The large rock dragon fixed his gaze on Feathering. 'You are not the first to know of the coming conflict. We are connected to all things in Starfell. We can sense everything that goes on in this world. We feel the change . . . like before. Something is coming . . . something that threatens us all.'

'Exactly! That's why we need your help!' cried Willow.

From behind them, a low hiss of smoke came from one of the other dragons. 'We should destroy the humans. They bring destruction to all creatures, big and small. They are a blight on this world.'

Willow flinched.

Another stony voice echoed these sentiments. 'We could stop them all – send the rocks rolling, form ourselves all across the land. End them once and for all.'

'Oh, me greedy aunt!' cried Oswin.

Peg, Twist and Willow gasped, 'No!'

With her heart thundering in her ears, Willow took a hesitant step towards the main rock dragon, her hands outstretched as if to calm him. 'Please don't judge us by one human. We can stop him – stop this war. If we all work together, no one needs to be wiped out.'

Feathering nodded his vast blue snout. 'I agree. Besides, I don't want to see dragons at war. And if you hurt my friends, there will be no other option.'

The rock dragon turned his head to face Feathering, considering the smaller beast's threat. He was at least ten times the size of the cloud dragon. Feathering didn't stand a chance.

Willow fought for air in her anxiety. Was this all one giant mistake? It was backfiring terribly . . . She looked at Twist, who seemed uncharacteristically cowed, her eyes full of fear. Peg was clutching the carpetbag, which was shaking, Oswin having zipped himself inside.

She took a deep breath, then swallowed. Feathering had mentioned that the rock dragons would help you if you offered a trade, something in return. She would do whatever it took to get them out of here and to stop Silas finding Llandunia and the elf staff.

Willow swallowed. 'Please help us. Please tell us where the kingdom was. I – I will give you whatever you want. Whatever you need me to trade.'

'No!' cried Oswin, peering at her from the hairy green bag, which he'd unzipped slightly.

'Don't do it!' cried Peg.

Twist scowled. 'Willow, we can find another way!'

But Willow shook her head. 'There is no other way. I can't bring the kingdom back without knowing where it was. Who knows how many other people's lives could be in danger? I'm just one person . . . It's fairer like this,' she said, though her voice shook along with her knees. She faced the dragon again. 'Tell me what you need.'

The rock dragon looked at her but didn't say anything for a long time. Then, 'You will pay a heavy price.'

Willow felt her knees give way slightly, and her stomach plummeted.

'Nooo!' moaned Oswin.

Willow's fear only increased as the enormous rock dragon moved suddenly closer to her and sniffed. She cried out as she felt herself being sucked towards his

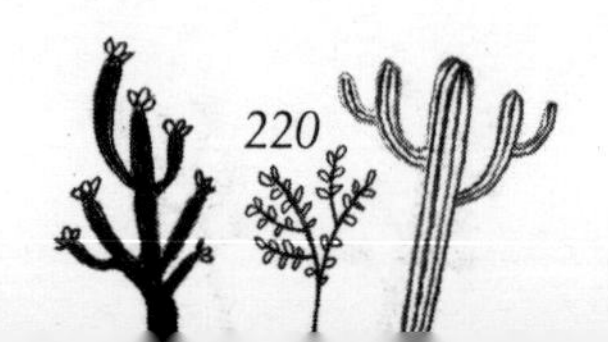

powerful stony nostrils, but Twist reached out and grabbed her by her cloak.

Willow wondered what they'd ask for . . . a memory? A name? The thought of losing any of her memories of Granny Flossy made her throat turn dry. As much as she was putting on a brave face, she was terrified of what they'd ask.

The rock dragon took another enormous sniff and Willow held on to Twist for dear life. Willow smelt something old and dry, like dust and heat and the echo of long ago.

Suddenly, the rock dragon blinked his large lichen eyes. He paused as he considered Willow in what seemed like surprise.

'You have been touched by magic,' he said. It wasn't a question.

Willow blinked. The dragon was right.

When she'd saved the missing day, there had been a moment in Wolkana when all had seemed lost – Silas had the powerful Lost Spells, he was shielded from their magic by a protective enchantment and Moreg's life force was trickling away. Willow had tried and tried to summon a spell scroll away from him, and suddenly magic itself heard her and decided to take a chance. It broke its own rules, released the protection round the spell and chose to help her. She'd managed to get the scroll and recite the counter-spell to restore the missing day because magic had seen something in Willow that day – something it hadn't seen in a long time. It had even granted her a second power – the ability to make things disappear – as a result.

'Y-you can tell?'

There was a hubbub from the other rock dragons, who inched closer to sniff at her. 'I can smell it too,' said one of the others.

There were nods of agreement all around. 'We must help her,' said one.

Willow felt a mix of hope and relief wash over her.

The big rock dragon was still considering her, still unwilling to let her know his decision just yet.

'Magic has put its trust in you. We are surprised. You are not very strong or powerful . . . It is an odd choice.'

'Yes,' said Willow, who couldn't help feeling just a little insulted, though it was probably best not to argue. Besides, she knew it was true. It *was* a bit odd. She didn't know why magic had put its faith in her, but she knew that she didn't want to let it down.

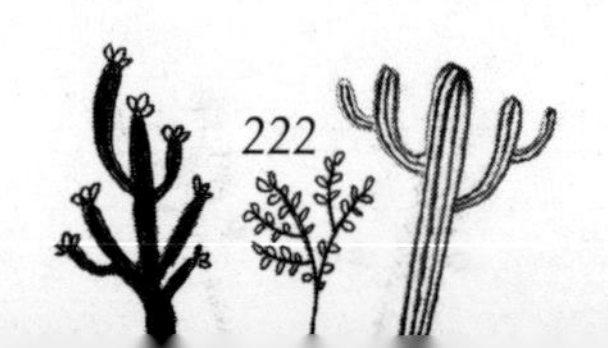

'Strength comes in all sizes.'

The rock dragon nodded. 'On that, we agree. A landslide often begins with a single rock, a pebble can cause a wave, a piece of grit can create a pearl . . . This we know. This we trust.'

He seemed to think for a while. Willow stood rooted to the spot, her heart in her mouth, until he spoke again.

'We were silent the last time. We didn't wish to get involved in human matters . . . but these are not human matters any more. Not when it threatens our world. And, if magic has placed its trust in you, so shall we. I no longer require a trade. I will tell you what happened.'

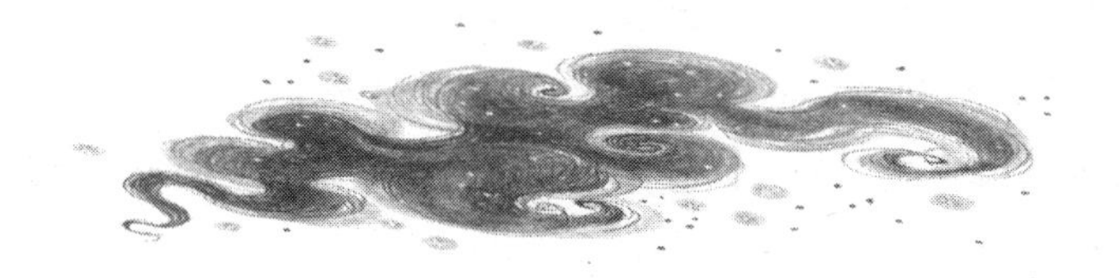

Long ago, when the moons lived side by side, there was a kingdom made of strange crystal in a spectrum of blues and greens edged with purple and pink. It was magnificent. It was a living organism that

responded to the wants and needs of its ruler, an elvish queen who loved the palace and her crystal kingdom like a family.

She was a benevolent ruler, entrusted with a vital task – to keep the balance in the world of Starfell.

People envied her this power. Particularly a human magician who named himself Wol and, in time, managed to make himself as powerful as he could by playing on the people's fears. He convinced those who were afraid of magic to follow him. He stole spells and used whatever methods he could to grow stronger. But there was one thing he knew would make him all-powerful. It was known as the elf staff. It could tap into the very source of magic itself and gift it to anyone and anything of its choosing. But it had a darker side too, which not many people knew: it could also take magic away.

Wol had become adept at disguises. He transformed himself into a deer and witnessed the queen as she used the staff in this way in the forest. As an old elf lay dying, the queen recited a ritual and used the staff to gently capture his magic and send it back into the ground round the body.

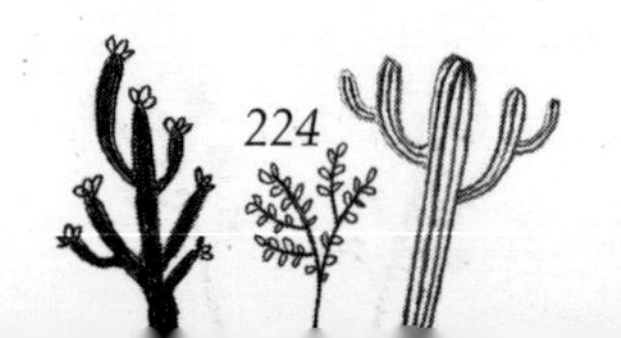

Wol's desire for the staff became an obsession, until one day he managed to break into the palace. He put all those inside it into a deep sleep, using a very powerful enchantment, and he took the queen's staff as his own.

Soon he began to make himself all-powerful. He started to call himself a god, and the Brothers of Wol grew ever stronger. He built a fortress that would keep out all magicians who might challenge him, and with the help of his non-magical Brothers, who believed they were doing what was right, he used the staff to strip the magic from all those he could. They did not see that the world was beginning to suffer, that people and animals, forests and lakes were suffering too . . .

But the elvish queen did. It took her a long time to manage to break into Wol's fortress, but she did so with the help of the dragon Vermora. The queen and the wizard fought, and Wol was injured.

The queen escaped, with the staff, on the back of the dragon. They flew to the forest that edged the beautiful elvish kingdom, and it was then that the queen knew she had to do something drastic to stop Wol and end the war . . . or it might mean the

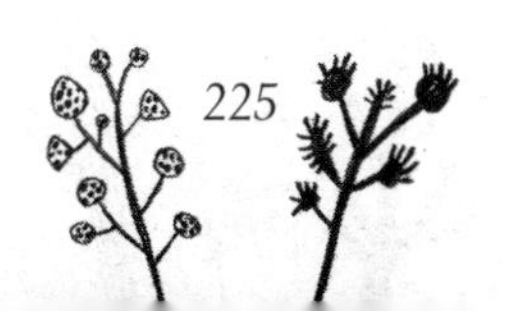

destruction of the world. He couldn't be allowed to use the staff for such a purpose ever again. No one could.

She called for her sisters and they spoke in quiet whispers. Afterwards, she sent them and all the elves away from Llandunia to find a new home. Then she began to run as men in long brown robes – Brothers of Wol – came for her, arrows ready.

The queen banged the staff on the ground. 'Vermora!' she cried, and the large, fiery red dragon canted in the sky and then landed near her once more.

'You need to take this,' she said, holding out a scroll, which she placed inside a leather satchel and hung round the dragon's neck. 'It will help the elves find this kingdom again, if they ever need to. Only an elf of my line will be able to decode it.'

Then she pressed her forehead against the dragon's snout.

'You must be a witness only, Vermora. Promise me?'

'A witness?' the dragon asked.

'To what will happen to me when they come.'

The dragon's eyes filled with pain. 'No!' she cried. 'I will NOT!'

'You must, Vermora. Our world depends upon it.

Llandunia and the staff must be hidden, and, for the enchantment to hold, I must go with them. I must take the staff back to the kingdom and ensure their protection. Lerisi.'

The dragon closed her eyes. 'Take it back,' she begged.

'Lerisi,' the queen whispered again.

'Don't . . . I cannot break it if you call upon a dragon vow.'

'Lerisi,' whispered the queen again, for the last time. Her eyes misted with tears. Then she touched Vermora's scaled face again and breathed, 'Farewell, my dearest friend.'

When Vermora's eyes opened, they shone with grief. The dragon watched as Queen Almefeira ran to the lake, the staff parting the water as she raced towards her kingdom on the other side.

From the forest, men in brown robes were following, arrows flying towards her.

The dragon roared helplessly in pain and rage as she watched an arrow strike the queen's chest. The sound Vermora made was as if her own heart had been pierced.

Almefeira stood in the parted lake, in front of the

kingdom, breathing shallowly from her wound. Then she struck the staff on the ground, so fiercely that the crystal orb let out a blast of pure energy. Above her head, the twin moons split apart and an earthquake began to rip the ground below. The ground started to crumble and sink, taking the lake, the queen and her kingdom ever lower, until they could be seen no more. The forest came next, the men falling into the swirling water that spun into the ground as if down a drain.

In the end, nothing was left behind except dry, barren ground that stretched for miles and miles, completely uninhabited but for rather large stony creatures who seemed utterly perplexed and a bit apprehensive about what had just happened . . .

The creatures remain there to this day. They have changed over time, becoming even more suspicious of magic, but they live in a place that you might know today as Troll Country.

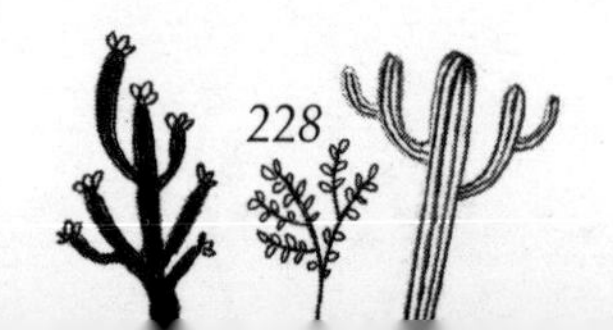

'I can't believes it,' said Oswin in horror.

'The vanished kingdom was in Troll Country,' breathed Willow.

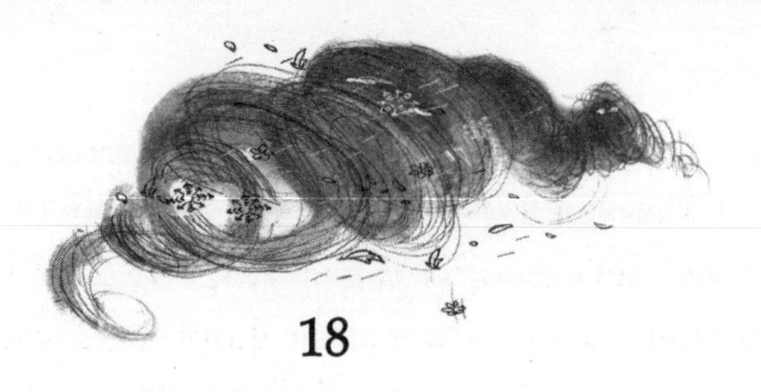

18

The Vanished Kingdom

Their tale told, the rock dragons began to disintegrate before their eyes, rocks and stones falling and scattering.

'Wait!' cried Willow.

'We have told you more than was asked,' called the voice of the enormous dragon.

The ground began to shake slightly once more as tiny rocks rattled across the surface. When at last they stopped, they formed into a very small, miniature rock dragon, with two small shadows for eyes.

Willow frowned.

'I think they mean for him to come with you,' whispered Peg.

'Oh, um, thank you,' said Willow, bending down. The creature jumped into her hands, then scuttled up her arm to rest on her shoulder. Willow looked at it.

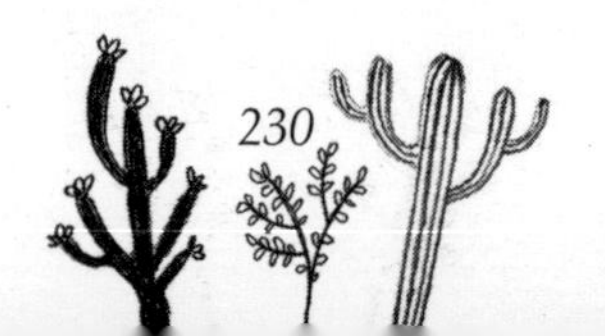

It blinked its dark eyes and then lay down, panting softly, as if it had run a very great distance.

'So lets me gets this straight,' said Oswin, peering out of the bag at the dusty space where the rock dragons had been and then looking at the tiny, now fast-asleep stone dragon on Willow's shoulder. **'The biggest beasts we ever met agree to helps us save the world . . . by sendin' us a rock newt?'** he harrumphed.

Willow looked back at him and nodded. That did seem to be the size of it.

'Well, at least now we know where Llandunia is,' she said. 'And that it's probably safe for me to summon it back. I mean, there's nothing in Troll Country.'

'Apart from the obvious,' said Feathering.

'Yeh . . . wonder how happy they wills be ter have a big kingdom pop up in their spot?'

'Well, it's just a risk we'll

have to take. I mean, we have to find it so we can get the staff before Silas does.'

They nodded.

'So, next stop Troll Country,' said Feathering, and they all climbed aboard – apart from Twist, who genuinely preferred to fly by tornado.

The sun was high in the sky as they flew through the misty Cloud Mountains and past winding lakes, over forests and towns. They stopped once for food, from a tree-market just outside the forest of Wisperia that was selling lemon buns and terhu rolls. The stallholder flew up into the canopy on her stained-glass wings at the sight of Feathering, and it took a while for them to convince her that the dragon wasn't in fact going to eat her but would quite fancy a bucket or two of currant buns. She reluctantly lowered some down to them, even though it was most of her stock for the day.

'Just a snack,' said Feathering, icing on his snout.

The tiny rock dragon simply nestled further into Willow's shoulder when she offered him some food, and she wondered if rocks ate anything. Water perhaps?

*

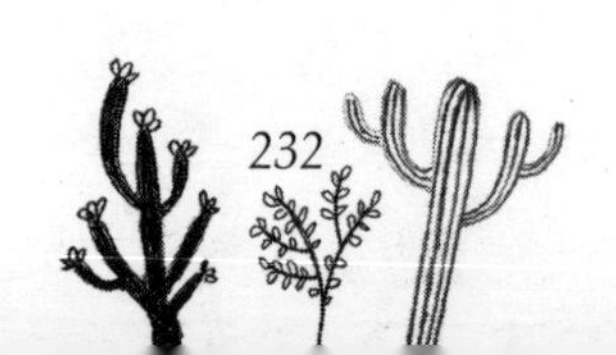

The sun was just beginning to set when they landed in Troll Country, a fiery pink beginning to paint the sky. Twist whirled down to join them, her eyes luminous as she took in the vast size of the area.

'How will we know where to summon the kingdom, Willow?' Peg asked, staring out at the bleak landscape.

'I'm not sure – it's so enormous – but it's mostly barren,' she said, looking out across the desert. 'I'd prefer to know exactly where it used to be before I try summoning it . . . but, well . . .'

Peg nodded. 'It's just too big to know, isn't it? Is it possible there are some signs left behind?'

'I could fly around and take a look?' offered Feathering. 'But I think, considering what the rock dragons told us, Almefeira took everything along with her when she hid the kingdom . . .'

Willow nodded. 'That's what I was thinking too. Perhaps I should just try to summon it somewhere where there are no troll huts. I can negotiate some things with my abilities, but unfortunately, I don't know about getting it perfectly in place . . . It might not be the exact spot where the kingdom used to be, but it's the best we can do . . .'

Twist had been traversing the area as Willow and Peg spoke, crossing over vast distances by tornado. She came back just in time to hear Willow's thoughts on where to summon the vanished kingdom.

'No,' she said, shaking her head vehemently. They stared at her in surprise and Twist explained. 'I can feel that elves have been here. It's faint, but it's elfsense, definitely.'

'Oh!' cried Willow and Peg together.

'Up ahead, it was a little stronger. Come with me,' she said.

They followed after her on foot for around ten minutes, and then the tall elf suddenly stopped, an odd look of amazement flashing across her face. 'I feel it more here.' She shook her head. 'Strange, isn't it?'

'Maybe not!' Willow gasped and pointed at the ground.

Where Twist walked, very, very faintly, the dusty ground had begun to glow green, like the elvish marble back in Lael.

The tiny rock dragon on Willow's shoulder scuttled down her arm and jumped on to the ground. He walked in circles, then came to a stop and looked back at them, nodding his minute head.

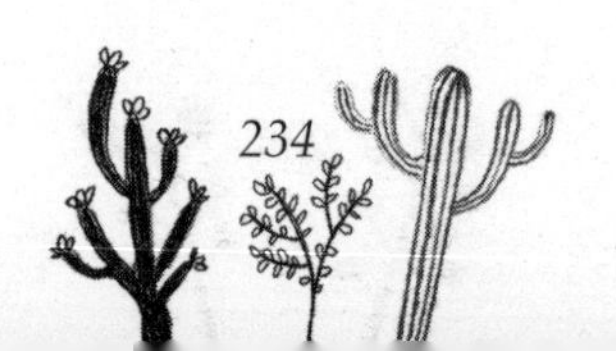

Twist looked from him to her booted feet. 'Great Starfell! Do you think . . . perhaps Llandunia is below here – is that what he's trying to tell us?'

Feathering nodded. 'I think so.'

Willow swallowed. Part of her was still terrified at the idea of bringing the kingdom back, but thankfully this open desert wasn't somewhere she would cause any real destruction. There were no homes or villages that could be affected. Besides, another part of her was grateful that they weren't too late – that Silas hadn't beaten them to it.

She looked at the others, a determined glint in her eye. 'I'm going to try finding it.'

They all nodded solemnly.

Willow closed her eyes, then raised her hand to the sky. The tiny rock dragon climbed back up her leg, on to her arm, then came to rest once more on her shoulder. Willow took a deep breath and tried to silence the voice at the back of her mind that wondered if she could even do this. Who was she to try? The biggest thing she'd ever made reappear was a kitchen, and that was by accident. Even the rock dragons were surprised that magic had chosen to trust her – they could sense that she wasn't particularly strong . . .

Then she shook that doubt away. She pictured Granny Flossy's warm eyes before she attempted a new potion, one for a day full of joy. 'Child, they are quick ter tell me not to try, that since me accident I fail more times than I succeed. But here's the thing . . . right now there's a chance I win. It's only when you don' try that you lose.'

The potion had gone wrong that time, but eventually she got it right – and besides, most days with Granny had been filled with moments of joy.

Willow took in another deep breath. *The only failure is not trying*, she reminded herself. Then she pictured finding the lost city, putting it back where it belonged. She painted the scene with her thoughts until finally, she saw it all in her mind's eye. She could feel it, like a secret whispering at the base of her skull.

It resisted at first – the kingdom – as if it were stuck and didn't want to move. But she pulled gently with her mind, imagining fresh air, crystal buildings, twin moons, a lake . . . and suddenly the kingdom began to respond. The feeling at the back of Willow's mind grew as Llandunia tentatively reached out for her mental picture. She was tempting it, cajoling it, with images of a different future.

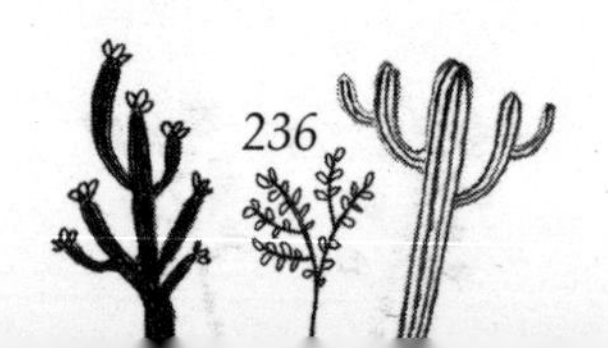

For the first time, Willow could truly feel the crystal – feel how the rock was sentient, how much it wanted to see the light again, to experience the dawn, the sky, the stars . . . She gave it that extra nudge it needed by showing it Twist, the other elves she'd seen in Lael and the incredible lumieres, weaving a whole tapestry for Llandunia of how life could be if it came back. She pulled a little harder, and this time it didn't resist.

And then suddenly a faint crack opened up in the earth.

'It's working!' cried Peg in amazement.

Willow felt a surge of hope. But she was careful to guide the kingdom, to show it that it could trust her. She gently encouraged it with her mind, and slowly but surely, it began to rise. Something sharp and pointed, and topped by what looked like two crescent moons, broke through the desert surface.

'It's a spire!' exclaimed Twist. 'I think it might be from the top of the palace! In the mural, it was the highest point in the kingdom.'

'Yes,' agreed Feathering. 'It is – I see it now!'

In the next moment, more of the kingdom began to rise from below the surface as the ground parted.

Willow and her friends scrambled backwards as Llandunia rose ever faster into the space around them.

'Oh no! Oh, me greedy aunt, 'tis comin' too fast!' cried Oswin.

'We need to get out of the way!' cried Twist.

Willow looked from the domed roof that was bursting through the ground to Twist and the others and nodded, eyes wide.

'Come on!' said Peg, running away from the kingdom that was erupting through the desert. But they weren't moving fast enough.

All too soon, the palace was almost halfway up, and Feathering was on the other side of it, too far away to get to them. As the ground continued to split apart and fall away, Willow and her friends fled, Skiron lending its support, but they weren't quick enough. As a flight of marble steps appeared beneath their feet, they tripped and fell – and then looked up in horror to see a rushing torrent of lake water coming straight for them.

There was nowhere to run.

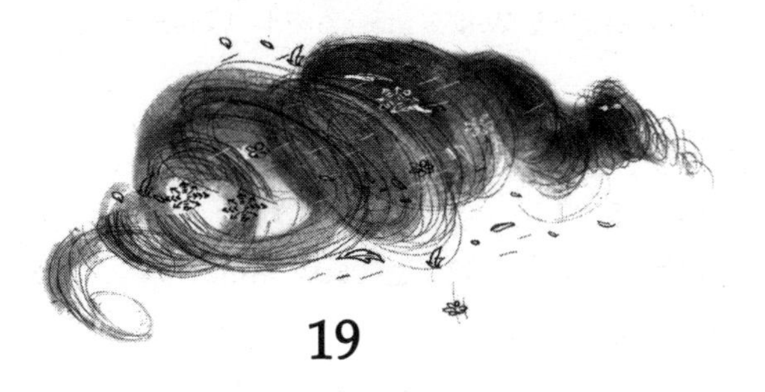

19

The Kingdom That Remembered

The water engulfed them all.

Willow's broom, Whisper, still strapped to her back, tore loose and drifted away.

Willow fought against the currents pulling her under. She needed air, but she could see the hairy green bag with Oswin inside a few feet away. He was struggling too as he tried and failed to unzip the bag, which had begun to sink. The rock dragon clung on to her collar as she dived towards Oswin and swam with all her might. Finally, she managed to reach the carpetbag and pull it towards her.

They broke the surface, Willow gasping for breath as she unzipped the bag so the kobold could do the same. He spluttered, coughing. Willow trod water as she held on to him and the bag, the water flowing

fast and attempting to pull them under once more. She looked up and saw Feathering flying over. He was trying to get to them but was whipping up more huge waves with his massive wings.

'We'll meet you on the shore, Feathering!' Willow

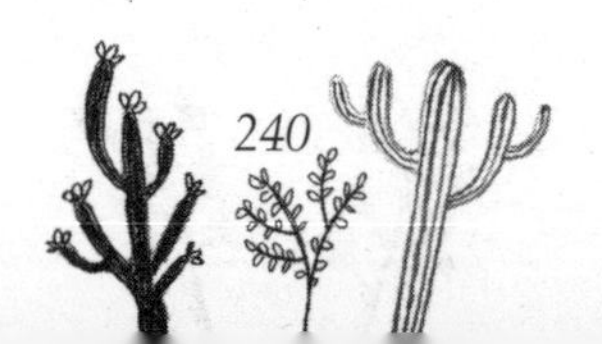

said, seeing the edge of the lake not far away, lapping at the steps of the palace.

The dragon nodded, realising he was making things worse.

Willow looked around for Peg and Twist.

'Up there,' said Oswin, pointing ahead. Willow felt a surge of relief to see her friends climbing out of the water and on to the palace steps.

The world had stopped moving at last, and the lake began to stabilise, the water growing still and calm.

It took a while, as Willow wasn't the strongest swimmer, but at last she dragged herself and Oswin to the lake edge and coughed up a torrent of water. It was some time before she was able to move the wet hair from her eyes and stare in awe at the vast, beautiful kingdom before her.

It was all shades of blue, green, purple and pink crystal, and the palace itself stood in the centre. It was huge and made up of various domed shapes with incredible carvings cut into the rock. The streets were marble, threaded with gold, and she could see many houses in the distance. Up above, Willow saw that Hezelboob and Jezelboob were reunited at last.

Peg and Twist helped them on to a long platform at the side of the stairs, where Feathering flew down to join them.

'You did it!' cried Twist.

Willow, still spluttering slightly, pushed herself

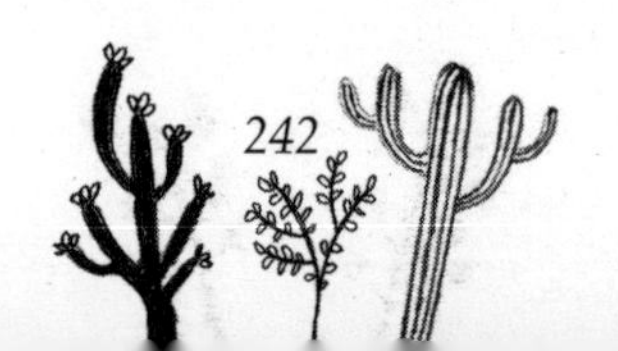

up off her knees and smiled. 'Yep. Sorry for almost killing everyone in the process.'

Peg grinned. 'To be fair, none of us thought that through properly.' They all laughed.

Twist pulled a piece of algae from Willow's hair. 'Come on, let's take a look!' she beamed, and they all followed her towards the palace.

As Twist walked up the stairs, the marble glowed green beneath her feet, and the kingdom seemed to come to life.

Willow, Peg and Oswin watched in awe as emblems on the vast palace began to wake up after centuries. Unlike the mosaic emblems in Lael, these were like statues carved into the crystal but even more lifelike. They raced over the walls – winged horses, dragons, water nymphs, elves, sprites, foxes and hounds. They had come from all directions, crossing over from some of the nearby houses to gather closer together for a better look.

'Salutations!'

'Hello there!'

'Friends, where are you?'

The sound became deafening as each one cried out excitedly, looking from Willow and her friends to the space behind them, expectant expressions on their crystal faces.

Twist and Willow suddenly felt desperately sad.

'I didn't know they could talk,' Willow whispered, her heart beginning to ache as the emblems crowded around one another, their expressions full of hope and longing.

'Neither did I,' Twist murmured as tears coursed down her face. 'They're looking for them.'

'Who?' asked Peg.

'The elves from before . . . The ones that left.'

'Oh,' he said, and his face fell. 'That's so sad.'

As one, the emblems and the crystal itself seemed to sense what Twist was feeling: regret, sorrow, pity. They began to realise that their old friends weren't coming back. There were keening wails. Willow felt tears flood her eyes as so many emblems crowded round the palace walls, looking for answers that wouldn't come. She watched helplessly as Twist sat down on the marble steps and began to cry.

Willow went to sit next to her, feeling awful. It was her fault all the crystal emblems were experiencing this! She had caused them this pain because she'd convinced the kingdom to return.

Her throat turned dry, and she tried to swallow, her lip wobbling. 'I'm so sorry,' she said to Twist, and as she sat down she felt the marble steps beneath her fingers. To her utter shock, it began to glow green like it had for the elf.

'Oh, Willow,' cried Twist, 'are you perhaps part elf?'

Willow shook her head, a tear running down her cheek as she looked up at the sad faces of the emblems, and she listened to the kingdom. She closed her eyes, and she felt it then: the pain . . . the loneliness . . . the terrible longing to be reunited with old friends. She didn't know what was happening exactly – but she could guess.

'It felt me, like I felt it, when I brought it here,' she said. 'It wants me to know that –' she took in a shuddery breath at the thought – 'it doesn't mind that I pushed for it to come back because it's better here than below . . . It's better to know what happened than to always wonder . . . to be trapped beneath the surface . . . *to be forgotten.*'

Willow wiped away the tears that just kept flowing as she felt the heart of the kingdom.

On some deep level, she knew exactly what Llandunia was feeling – because it was the same thing she'd felt after the missing day was restored, when she'd discovered that Granny Flossy had died. It had been excruciating, realising that she was gone, but somehow the not knowing – the idea of simply forgetting – was so much worse.

Twist wiped her eyes. Even Peg was welling up.

'That's very true,' said Feathering, 'though,

Llandunia, you have never been forgotten.'

'And you can have a new life,' said Twist, 'and make new memories.'

Willow took a deep breath and squared her shoulders. They would only have that – a new life filled with new memories – if they found what they were looking for and prevented Silas from destroying all their futures.

'We need to find the elf staff,' she said, standing up.

Twist nodded. 'You're right.'

Her words, however, caused a hubbub from the emblems, as they each tried to speak at once.

A winged horse reared up on its hindquarters. 'You cannot go looking for the elf staff!'

A water nymph shook her head, then dived into the crystal as if it were water. She reappeared on another wall and cried, 'It's why she buried us. Leave it where it lies.'

More emblems shouted much the same warnings. Willow and the others stared at them in shock.

'Do you know where it is?' she asked.

A fox stared at her mutely. A dog looked at the marble steps instead of meeting her eyes and said, 'No . . .'

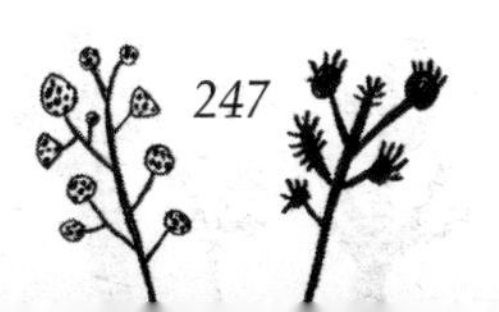

Twist frowned. 'You're lying,' she breathed.

'Don't ask it of him,' said an elf emblem, approaching from one of the houses up ahead on a long marble road. She was made of blue and green crystal and moved through the street and then on to the palace wall with ease, like she was a shadow.

'But you know where it is?' asked Twist.

She nodded.

'Please, we only want it so we can protect it. Someone is coming, someone powerful – and, if he gets here, it will be too late,' said Twist.

The elf and the other emblems stopped to stare at them, then finally they all nodded. Perhaps, thought Willow, they could sense that Twist was telling the truth.

The elf emblem pointed towards the lake. 'It is in there.'

'Thank you,' said Willow, and she turned to walk back down the palace steps. The others followed.

Willow stopped at the edge of the lake to close her eyes, and then she began once more to search for the staff with her mind.

Like there had been at Howling House, there was a blast, like an electric current, and she flew over backwards.

'Willow, are you all right?' cried Twist, rushing towards her.

Willow blew out her cheeks, then stood up. 'Fine.' She closed her eyes once more, to try again.

'Oh, me greedy aunt,' moaned Oswin, from near her feet. He'd opened the carpetbag and stood it upside down to dry out. **'I can'ts lewk.'**

Willow took a deep breath, planting her feet wide apart. Twist held on to her to lend her strength, and Willow shot her a grateful smile before concentrating on the staff.

Electrical blast after electrical blast rocked them. Then, suddenly, a tall, spiralled stick began to break the surface and rise from the lake.

Willow and the others cried out jubilantly . . . only to then gasp in shock as something else emerged – something with scales and fierce claws, something that was clutching the elf staff with all its might and looked utterly furious to boot. It was a fearsome creature from below. Its hair and beard were made of hundreds of tiny serpents, and its eyes and fish-like tail were gold.

''Tis a merman!' cried Oswin.

Willow nodded. The tiny rock dragon shifted

position on her shoulder, staring at the lake creature with interest.

'Please,' Willow called to the merman. 'Someone dangerous knows where to find you. We need to take this staff, to protect it from him.'

But it didn't look like the merman was in the mood to talk or to release the staff. Instead, he clung on tighter and sent another powerful electric current towards her.

'Well, that answers that,' said Willow with a sigh.

'Let me try something,' said Twist fiercely, with a crackle of her own storm energy. She released a bolt of lightning towards the merman, and Willow tried to summon the staff with her magic, hoping to catch him when he was distracted. But Twist only seemed to have angered him. In response, the creature's next electric shock was stronger than ever, blasting Willow so far off her feet that Skiron had to break her fall.

'Oh, he's never going to let it go!' cried Willow. 'Do you think the water nymph emblem can help us?'

'I am bound to the walls – I cannot enter the lake,' called the emblem behind them. 'And while I trust your purpose, I am wary of your plan.'

Willow groaned and turned to her friends in despair.

Then Oswin nodded, as if he had done some serious thinking . . . He padded away from the wet carpetbag, made his way slowly to Willow's side and faced the lake. Then he hissed at the merman, his fur standing on end. In that moment, he looked even more like a cat than he ever had in his whole life.

The creature flinched. For just a moment, the electric current he was transmitting sputtered and then grew strong once more. Twist held on to Willow as she was nearly blasted off her feet again.

'Oswin!' Willow gasped, guessing his plan. 'Try it again!'

The kobold took a deep breath, closed his eyes and muttered, **'The fings I do fer yew.'** Then he squared his shoulders, dashed towards the water and, holding out both his front paws threateningly, made a pretty bad attempt at a *miaow* . . .

The merman recoiled. It was just for a split second, but it was all Willow needed, and she summoned the staff towards her with all her might. From the lake, there was a deep roar of vengeance, and the merman released another bolt of electricity, knocking them

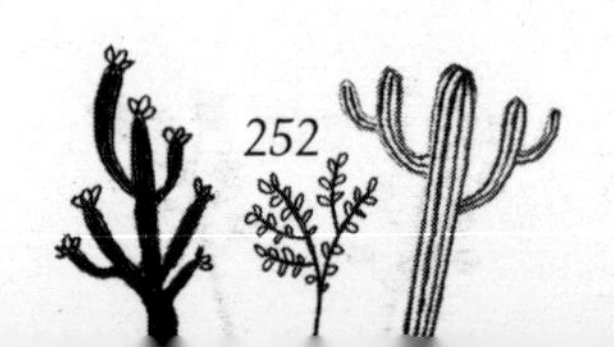

all off their feet. Willow and Twist crashed back on to the steps, but not before Willow felt something enormous, and wet, land in her outstretched hands.

'I've got it!' she cried.

There were cheers from Peg, Twist and Feathering, and the merman retreated to the depths of the lake once more.

Willow stood up awkwardly, wincing, but brandishing the heavy staff in triumph. She could feel the colossal power and energy radiating from it.

'Oswin, you're amazing, thank you!' she said.

'Fanks,' he said. Then he shot them all a hard look. **'But, jes ter be clear, I is NOT a cat.'**

They all nodded seriously – though Twist's lips did shake with suppressed laughter.

'But you were brilliant to make him think it,' said Peg, who was perhaps remembering the kobold's story about how his appearance had resulted in him nearly being married off to a mer-princess.

The kobold shrugged, but they could detect what almost looked like a catlike smirk.

Suddenly, there was the sound of someone clapping.

Willow looked at her friends – only they'd all turned pale and were staring back in the direction of the lake.

'Right on time,' said a cold voice from behind Willow.

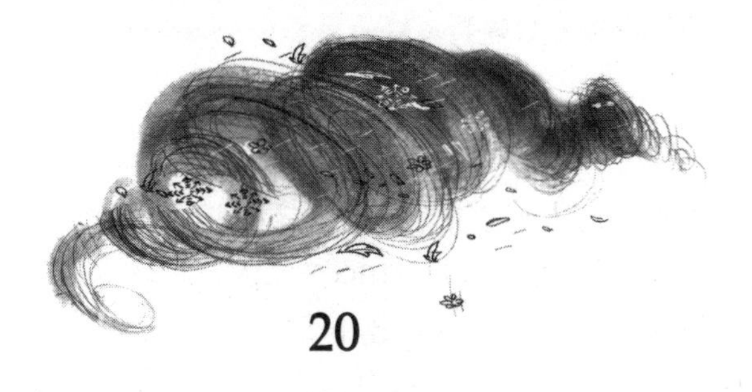

20

The High Master's Plan

Willow's heart started to thud.

Silas.

He was standing on a small boat in the water, surrounded by half a dozen Brothers. Though no one was steering, they were moving at great speed towards Willow and her friends. Even from her position on the palace steps, she could see Silas's smile, which was cold and terrible.

All too soon, the boat stopped at the water's edge, and he took a casual step on to the platform, his wide smile firmly in place.

'Oh no,' whispered Oswin.

Silas was followed by his faithful Brothers. Each one had glazed eyes – from the Gerful chalk, Willow realised. Worse still, she spotted that one of them was holding a pair of glowing blue manacles.

She blinked in horror. They were outnumbered.

'I must say,' Silas said, 'you have behaved exactly according to plan. Who would have thought when we first met all those months ago that the little girl who tried to thwart me would play such a big part in my success? I really must thank you.'

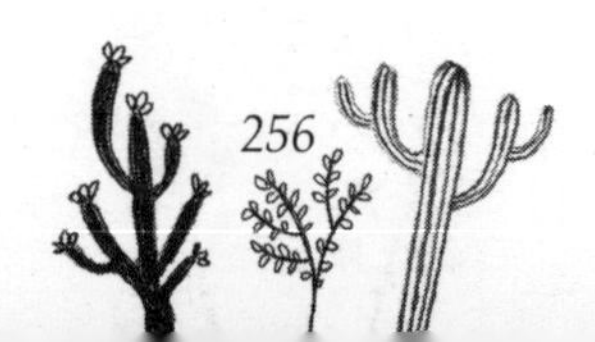

Willow's heart was roaring in her chest. She frowned in confusion. 'Thank me for what?'

He grinned. 'For this! Bringing the kingdom of Llandunia to me. I must confess that even with all the Lost Spells at my disposal, I wasn't sure how I was going to locate it. And then I realised I'd never need to.' He took out something from his long black robe. It was a folded copy of the *Grimoire Gazette*. His eyes flashed in amusement. 'I'd just let you follow the breadcrumbs . . . and you'd end up doing it all for me.'

Willow paled. 'But the scroll from Library . . . the one you stole . . . ?'

'Yes, I hoped that the infamous scroll said to contain the whereabouts of the vanished kingdom would catch your attention. I did steal it – well, one of my followers did anyway. Of course, I was unable to translate it – but that wasn't necessary, my dear. All I needed was for you to *think* I could. Oh, it was so wonderful to see how easily you played along. I'm much obliged.'

'Skiron, blow!' cried Twist, and the wintry wind began to gust itself into a frenzy.

Silas staggered against the unexpected gale as it whipped his black robes round him.

Immediately, two brainwashed Brothers advanced on Willow and, reacting quickly, she tightened her grip on the staff and started to race up the palace steps.

Remembering she'd managed to lose her broom when Llandunia had reappeared, she held out her other hand and tried to summon it. Instead, she was met with the blast of yet another electric current and tripped over. She whirled round to see the merman back at the surface of the lake, holding on to Whisper, a cruel grin on his face.

'Blast!' she cried, getting up gingerly and hurrying up the remaining steps towards the palace.

A few of the emblems came racing over the walls, shouting instructions – though many chastened her about summoning the staff in the first place.

'Fly away!' said the hound. But Willow couldn't.

'Summon your army!' cried the winged horse. But Willow didn't have one.

She looked behind her and saw that Twist had sent a bolt of lightning after the group of Brothers who were trying to corner Willow.

'Thank you!' cried Willow, just as thunder started to boom out of the elf's mouth, and rain lashed down from the sky. Maybe she *did* have a

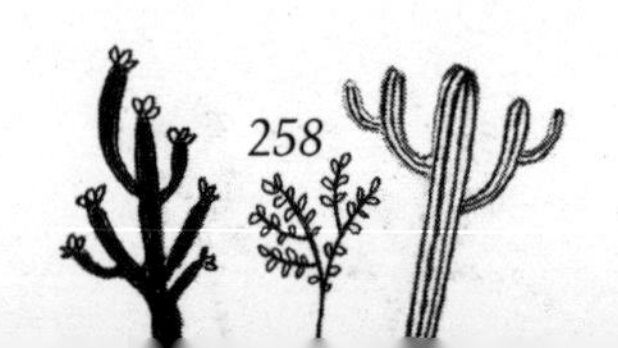

small army, she thought, just as Feathering roared, launching himself at Silas, and the two began to do battle.

Silas's magic bounced off the beast's thick hide. But then Willow watched in horror as Silas made some complicated gesture, and Feathering was flung against the palace and transformed into a crystal emblem of a dragon, trapped inside the wall behind him.

'Feathering, no!' cried Willow, racing towards him.

'It won't hold him long,' reassured the winged horse emblem. 'It's illusory magic – a very old trick. He's just made the beast – and us – *think* he's crystal.'

'Are you sure?'

The winged horse nodded. 'I'll try to convince him to wake up. Go, run,' he said, and Willow did.

She ran towards the palace doors, thinking that if she could just get out of sight inside, she could try to make the staff disappear . . . She'd need to concentrate.

There was a cry from behind, and Willow turned to find that the Brothers were recovering and heading towards her again. Oswin swatted at one of them, but more seemed to be appearing from nowhere.

'Seize her!' cried Silas. 'Get that staff!'

Willow ducked out of their way, and Twist tried once again to hold off the Brothers with her weather magic. But Silas reached inside his robe and took out a small scroll that Willow recognised as one of the ancient Lost Spells. He read it fast.

Suddenly, there was a flash of bright yellow light, and Twist began to struggle as if she were drowning . . . but drowning in air.

Willow swung the staff round at one of the Brothers, knocking him off his feet. Peg and Oswin raced up the steps after her. Peg managed to punch one of the Brothers, while Oswin launched himself at another, scratching him on the nose. He was soon shaken off, and his small furry body was flung down the steps – but Oswin landed on his feet and once again threw himself into the fray.

Willow aimed another blow at one of the brainwashed Brothers who was coming at her once again, despite a nasty lump forming on his head.

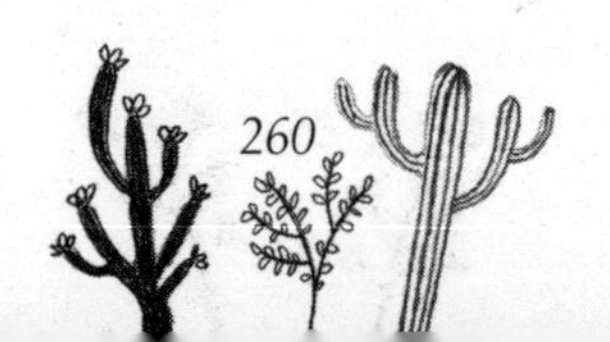

Another one had managed to restrain Peg, pinning his body to the floor.

Undeterred by the blows raining down on them, three managed to grab hold of Willow as she kicked and thrashed and waved the staff around, and one finally tore it from her hands. Oswin dived at him, only to bc flung backwards down the steps once more. He tried to stand up, but this time he collapsed, making a soft mewling sound.

Willow's heart dived into her mouth.

'No!' she screamed as the Brother who'd torn the staff from her hands snapped a pair of glowing manacles roughly on to her wrists.

Willow fought hard, battling against her restraints, but they were locked in place. She struggled to her knees, her heart thundering in her chest. She watched in utter horror as, one by one, the Brothers passed the staff between them to Silas.

Twist pointed frantically at the scroll on the ground beside Oswin as she fought for air. 'Say the reverse,' she tried to shout, but the

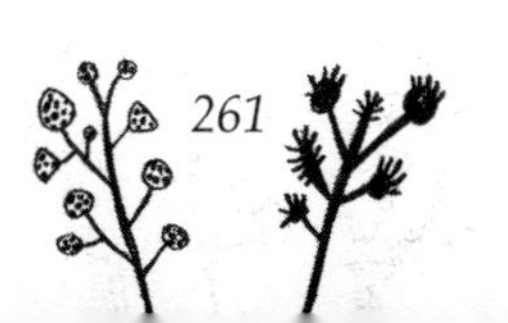

kobold couldn't understand her as her strangled voice sounded like it was coming from deep underwater.

'Turn it round, Oswin!' cried Willow. 'Say what's on the back!'

Oswin quickly grabbed it and read out,

'Water to air,
Breath and life,
Meet once more,
Restore the balance fair.'

Twist was released at last, and she fell to her knees, gasping for breath.

'Thank you, Oswin,' she cried.

The kobold nodded, then paled as he looked from Twist to Silas. They all turned in horror as Silas held the staff in his hands, grinning widely.

Willow felt her heartbeat roaring in her ears. Silas had won!

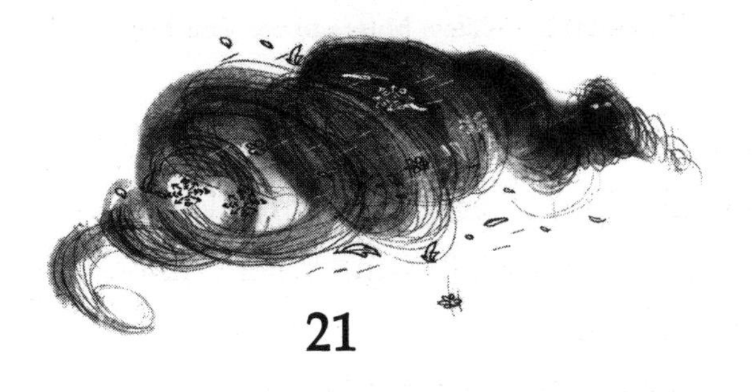

21

Troll Army

Silas raised the staff to the sky, a terrible look of triumph on his face.

Twist tried to send a bolt of lightning at him, but nothing happened. 'I'm too weak,' she cried.

Willow started to hyperventilate. Silas was going to steal all their magic. They had failed! There were spots before her eyes as she gasped for breath in her panic.

'Summon your army!' cried the winged horse again.

Willow thought, foolishly, that their army was defeated. Silas was about to bring about utter destruction . . . until suddenly she looked up and blinked. Was the emblem hound referring to something else? Did he know what Moreg had told her, or was he just speaking nonsense? It didn't matter. She could kiss the crystal dog either way, as his words

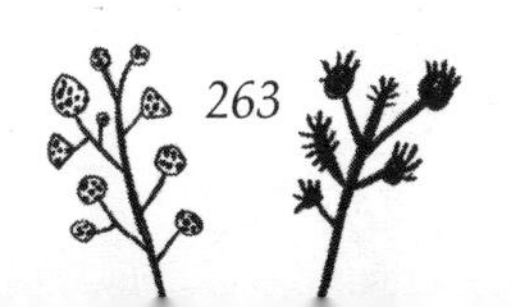

had sparked something in her. She sat up fast and turned to look down the steps at Oswin.

'The whistle!'

'The wissel?' he said. Then suddenly his eyes widened. He nodded quickly and then, with an enormous struggle, he half padded, half crawled to the upside-down carpetbag that had been left to dry. Socks and nightdresses and several biscuits went flying, till he found something small and hard buried at the bottom of the bag. He held it to his mouth and blew. The whistle let out a sharp, shrill cry that made them all wince.

Even Silas lowered the staff to peer around in surprise.

For a moment, nothing happened, and then . . . from far away, they could hear an ENORMOUS BOOM.

The ground began to shake. The water in the lake started to churn. It sounded like thunder or an earthquake.

'What on Starfell?' cried Silas.

Beyond the lake, whirling banks of dust clouds were forming in the air.

Something was coming. Something FAST.

Something LOUD and THUNDEROUS.

BOOM.

BOOM.

BOOM.

Despite the Gerful chalk, a few of the Brothers looked suddenly terrified. They scrambled up the steps as Silas called, 'Steady! Remain steady!' Though even he appeared to have lost some of his bravado, because suddenly they could all see what was coming: enormous creatures, as tall as the buildings, wider than several trees.

'Oh Wol!' cried Twist and Peg, their eyes wide in fright.

The huge shapes ran, leaving behind great dents in the ground. Their legs made short work of the lake, which barely reached their thighs. Their bodies were made of stone, their teeth covered with moss. They wore human bones as jewellery, and, despite the fact that their knuckles were the size of bricks,

they also carried studded clubs that they dragged menacingly through the water, their eyes fixed on them.

The creatures reached Willow and Oswin in a cloud of dust, followed by a wave of water that made everyone cough and splutter.

A sixteen-foot troll they knew as Verushka turned to Oswin. 'You have summoned us?'

Suddenly, Willow spotted another troll behind the great warrior. 'Calamity!' she shouted.

'Willow!' cried her friend, a smaller troll of around her own age. Calamity made her way towards Willow and, seeing the manacles on her wrists, she snapped them off immediately. 'You used the whistle!' she said.

Willow nodded. 'We need your help! Please stop them!' She pointed at Silas and the Brothers, who were staring at the trolls, frozen in disbelief.

Calamity nodded. 'My clan doesn't remember you, but they'll keep their word. No one gets a whistle unless it's been handed over by a troll – it's an ancient custom.' Then she turned to Verushka and the other trolls. She spoke quietly for a moment, and then they all nodded.

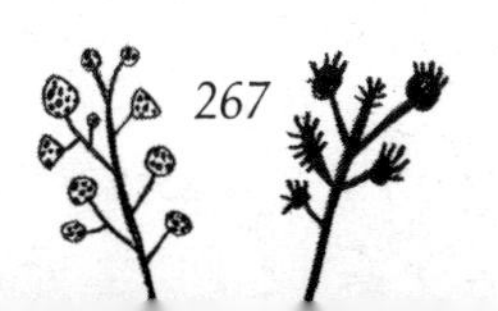

'Go after them,' said Verushka, pointing at the Brothers, who were now attempting to flee.

The trolls nodded. It was clear they didn't remember giving Willow the whistle, but the fact Oswin had blown it seemed like proof enough and meant they could rely on their help.

The trolls began to scatter, seizing the stunned Brothers in their fists and going after Silas. But he dashed down a street. He darted out of the way of one troll, who crashed into the side of a house. There was the heartbreaking sound of crystal shattering, and Silas managed to get away just in time. Willow could see him, holding the staff high in the air. He was preparing to use it!

'Oswin, hiss at the water again!' she cried.

He frowned but limped as quickly as he could towards the lake and hissed. There was an electrical blast, and Willow staggered back, but not before she held her broom, Whisper, in her hands. 'Thank you,' she called, jumping on and shooting after Silas. The superfast Stealth-Racer broom caught up and she dived at him, her hands reaching for the staff.

'What the—?' he said in surprise, pushing her back, but she clung on to the staff with all her might.

He took one hand off the staff to reach inside his pocket. Willow closed her eyes for a second, and the small box that had been inside his robes was in her left hand.

'You're forgetting that these are known as the *Lost* Spells,' she said, and threw them on to the ground.

He glared at her and pushed her back once more, trying to wrestle the staff out of her grip.

Willow struggled with Silas as he tried to fling her off, but she clamped her hands on to the staff and managed to hold on for dear life . . . She tried to think of making the staff vanish to get it away from Silas, but the air was dusty and it was making her eyes itch. At that exact moment . . . she sneezed.

And *she* vanished – taking the staff with her.

Silas roared in anger.

But Willow reappeared a second later, still on her broom, only a few feet away. 'Oh Wol!' she cried, wishing she had a better command of her new power.

Silas took a running leap towards her, knocking her off Whisper. The staff fell out of her hands, and they both scrambled after it, each one managing once again to grab a hold. Willow had caught the staff's iron half-moon, and she held on with all her strength. But Silas was stronger – far stronger – and, as she watched, he smiled terribly, clamped his hands over hers and began to twist the iron half-moon until the crystal turned black.

'Oh, I shall enjoy this,' he said. 'It makes sense, really, for it to come from you first.'

Willow felt a sudden jolt, and a tingling all through her body, like she'd been stung. The more she clung on, the weaker she became, but she was determined not to let go . . . She held on, fighting as black spots started to dance before her eyes. She staggered on to her knees, pulling the iron half-moon back towards her with the last bit of her strength . . . She pulled and pulled, twisting it until the crystal turned from black to white.

Then suddenly Willow felt something give way, but she wasn't sure what. She staggered back, and the tiny

rock dragon from her shoulder jumped to the ground. Her eyes desperately wanted to close in a sudden, crushing fatigue, but the look of triumph that faltered for a moment on Silas's face kept her holding on.

The earth started to rumble and shake as rocks began to roll towards the tiny dragon.

Silas looked from Willow, nearly unconscious on the ground, to the stones round him in confusion. Willow crawled away as fast as she could, using her last reserves of energy.

More and more rocks and pebbles appeared, collecting together until the once small dragon had grown enormous in size, shaping into the giant beast they had met in the Cloud Mountains.

It turned to Silas and roared. A wave of dust clouded the air, and Silas took an involuntary step backwards.

'I don' believes it!' cried Oswin. **'The rock newt wos the giant all this times!'**

Silas aimed the staff at the dragon, but the orb was still white, and nothing happened. Instead, the rock dragon opened its cavernous mouth, and Silas was engulfed. In moments, the moving, scattering rock disappeared, taking Silas along with it.

Willow watched through eyes glazed with fatigue, too weak to even lift her head from the ground. She heard the cheers. She heard the triumphant calls of the trolls and the horrified cries of the Brothers. She saw Feathering, thankfully released from his enchantment and fully restored, and heard him explaining to the others that the rock dragons would take Silas away to the Cloud Mountains . . . where they would keep him imprisoned.

But she couldn't find the words to respond. She could barely move. It would be good, she thought, to just rest a little while . . .

She felt weak – so very weak.

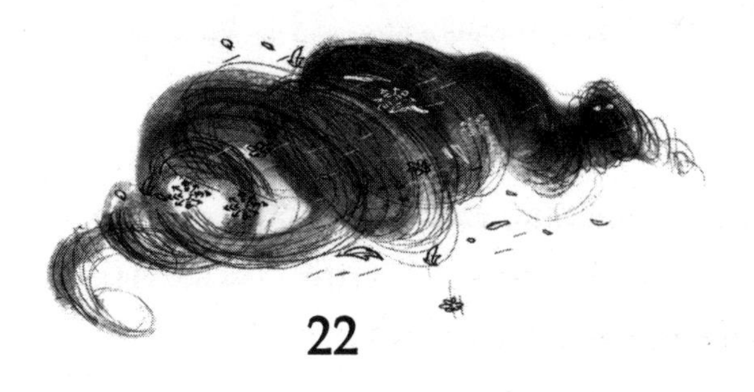

22

The Iron Moon

It had been a long journey back home, even though Feathering had flown as quickly as he could. Willow had been so tired and groggy, it had felt like her head was underwater or that everything was happening in a kind of dream, and she'd fallen into a deep sleep at some point before being delivered home.

When Willow woke up a week later, she still felt unbearably tired, but she was surprised nonetheless to find that she was clutching something in her fist . . . something no one had been able to prise from her fingers. She looked at it in surprise – it was the iron half-moon from the staff. She frowned. Had she somehow managed to wrench it off? How?

She could hear Oswin's faint snores coming from

the foot of her bed. She tried to sit up, but it was hard. She still felt impossibly weak.

To her surprise, she saw that Moreg Vaine was standing at the end of the bed.

Willow blinked, wondering if she were still dreaming.

There was a very faint, **'Oh no,'** from the kobold, who had woken when Willow stirred.

'You're awake,' said the witch. 'At last.'

'You're here,' said Willow. Though she was groggy and her mouth was dry, she felt a flicker of happiness spread through her at the thought.

'I am. I would have come sooner, but I'm afraid Silas managed to block my visions.'

Willow tried again to sit up, and the witch helped her raise herself on her pillows. 'What – how?' she asked in shock.

'He used a clouded eye, of all things – the very one that used to belong to your friend Holloway.'

Willow gasped. 'But I thought it was useless? He said it just made the world and his mood clouded. That's why he traded it.'

'Their purpose is not common knowledge, but if you have a clouded eye or carry one on your person,

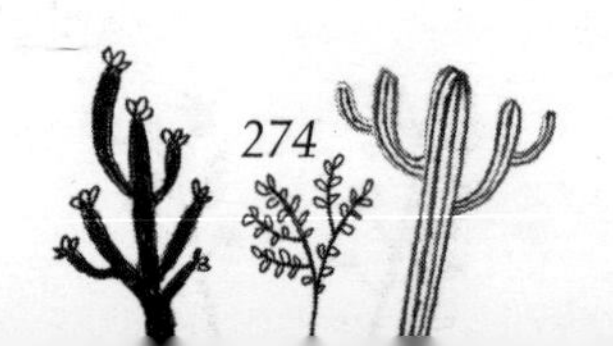

it warps a seer's visions of your future. I don't think Holloway or even Rubix knew this. Every time my visions turned towards you, and therefore Silas, everything began to get muddy . . . I started to think that it meant the problem was me, and the best thing I could do was not to come near and interfere. It was only later, when I read that the eye had been stolen from Rubix, that I figured out what had happened. Alas, I discovered it too late. But it's why I'm here now.'

'It's not too late,' said Willow.

'Never,' agreed Moreg. 'Your friends have filled me in on all that has happened. Your sisters too – I believe they are most proud.'

Willow frowned, then she looked around, realising that she was, in fact, in Camille's bed, which was bigger than her own. She was also wearing one of Juniper's jumpers. They must have tended her while she slept, she realised.

'I asked to speak to you as soon as you awoke. I hope you don't mind.'

Willow shook her head.

'We are all very proud of you.'

Willow felt tears smart in her eyes. She looked

away. They were words she'd longed to hear – to feel that her family, that Moreg Vaine, could be proud of her . . . But all she felt right then was a deep sense of shame. Her lip wobbled as all the events of the past few days overwhelmed her. 'No . . . you shouldn't be! I don't deserve it. I – messed up. I was the biggest fool. I shouldn't have brought Llandunia back.' She thought of all the people's lives she'd put at risk, and a tear slipped down her cheek. 'It was all my fault.'

Moreg's dark eyes snapped fire, and she clutched Willow's hand firmly. 'No! Do you hear me? I won't have that. Silas was playing a powerful game – and we were all his pawns. Your friend Twist is also riddled with guilt. She feels that if she hadn't come to find you and tell you about the kingdom, you might never have been put through this.'

Willow frowned. She'd never blame Twist.

'It doesn't matter how it happened. The important thing is that you all defeated Silas – for now,' said Moreg.

'For now?' Willow remembered him disappearing into the rock dragon's mouth and what Feathering had said – that they would hold him captive in the Cloud Mountains.

'I think, maybe, you already suspect what's happened? What he's done to you?'

Willow clutched the piece of iron in her palm. There was something tugging at her mind . . . something hard and painful that made her want to sob in anguish.

Perhaps if she didn't say it aloud, it wouldn't be true. It was even worse than the shame she felt. This was loss and grief . . . it felt raw and agonising, and a big part of her didn't even want to think of it, let alone admit it.

Moreg's face was grave even as she nodded kindly, encouraging Willow to speak aloud what seemed unspeakable.

Willow took a deep breath, tears filling her eyes as the horror of it washed over her. 'He took it, didn't he? My magic.'

That was why she felt so weak, so ill . . . A part of her had been stripped away.

She couldn't see for the tears that were falling now, fresh and fast.

She'd wished so much to be like her sisters – to be powerful, to be respected, to be admired . . . to have an ability that didn't cause people to view her as the 'least powerful sister'. And now she would give anything, anything at all, to have her simple, wondrous power back.

She took a shuddery breath and closed her eyes. Moreg patted her hand. 'I'm so sorry, but yes, he did. Unfortunately, in the moment Silas had the staff and turned it black, he took your magic from you. And, in doing so, he unintentionally took the one power he would need to escape the rock dragons.'

Willow blinked, then sighed. 'The ability to disappear. He knows I can do it because he saw me vanish when I tried to make the staff disappear.'

Moreg nodded. 'And he will come back with the elf staff.'

Willow sat back and closed her eyes. Then somehow,

despite everything, a small, triumphant smile flitted across her face. 'It won't work, though. Not without this.' Willow held up the iron half-moon.

Moreg looked at it and frowned. Her eyes turned white, then back to black. She gave a small, amazed laugh. 'Oh, you marvel! No, it won't. Not for its dark purposes.'

Willow beamed, relief flooding through her.

'Silas might have the staff – for now – but what you and your friends have achieved cannot be underestimated. At every turn, you have foiled his plans. You have soldiered on, even when none of our magical folk wanted to believe that a threat was coming. Even as they questioned your sanity, you persevered – knowing that you faced certain danger but doing the right thing regardless. You have shown true courage and integrity, and because of you and Twist, the children of Starfell have been saved so much pain – the pain that you now face yourself.'

'I must have used the very last drops of my magic to make this disappear from the staff!' Willow realised, staring at the iron half-moon.

Moreg nodded. 'You sacrificed your magic, to help save everyone else's.' The witch discreetly wiped her eyes. 'But it won't be for long, Willow. If we get the staff back, we can get your magic back too.'

Willow stared up at her, a curl of hope expanding in her chest. Moreg's words washed over her like a balm. Silas might think he'd won – but it wasn't over, not yet. Despite his cruel trick, she *had* achieved something. They all had. And she had made two incredible new friends in Twist and Peg, who she couldn't wait to see again. She'd get her magic back if it was the last thing she did. And right now that seemed, somehow, possible.

There was the sound of footsteps behind Moreg, and Willow's sisters, mother and father crowded into the room.

'You're awake!'

'Thank you for sending Thundera to save us!' cried Camille. 'She burnt down part of Wolkana and the Brothers had to let most of us go.'

'Did you know they used Gerful chalk on us? I can't believe we sent you to that school!' cried her father.

Oswin handed Willow a biscuit. **'Jes imagine all the time we could 'ave saved if they jes believed us from the start.'**

Willow took it and let out a small laugh.

To her astonishment, her mother ruffled the kobold's fur and grinned. 'Your cat might actually have a point.'

'Oh, fer the last time, despite 'AVING TER PRETEND fer likes a second that I is one to save our skins . . . I IS STILL *NOT* A BLOOMIN' CAT!'

Willow grinned, in spite of everything that had happened. Then she fished out the StoryPass from her pocket. She wasn't all that surprised that it was currently pointing to '*One Might Have Suspected as Such*'.

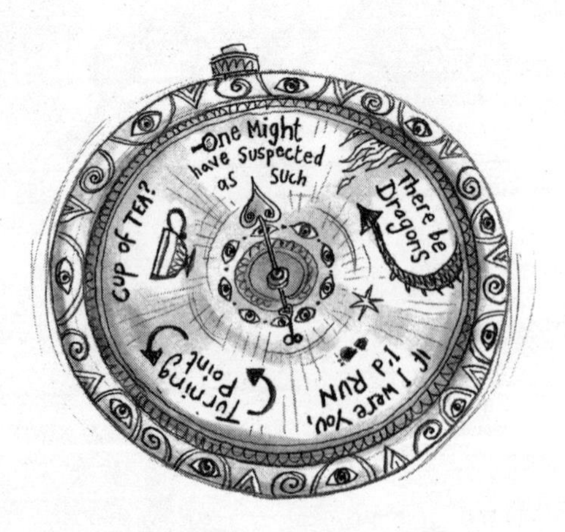

Acknowledgements

I think it is easy to look at a name on a cover and think that is where everything stops and starts, and the truth is, it's only really where things begin. So much hard work goes into bringing a story into the world, and from the people whose names don't get to go on the cover – yet they should.

I wrote the first, rough draft before the initial 2020 lockdown and, afterwards, I found that trying to bring the story to life during the Covid-19 pandemic was incredibly difficult. The only reason it is a book at all is thanks to my incredibly kind, patient and encouraging editors, Harriet Wilson and Julia Sanderson, who helped me when I couldn't see the wood for the trees; putting their brains together and gently guiding me to reshape and chisel the story until it became a book that I was eventually proud of. I couldn't have done it without you; I feel incredibly blessed to work with you. Your support and love for Starfell has made it such a joy.

I will never really know what I did in a past life to deserve my wonderful agent, Helen Boyle, who is the first person who reads my stories and offers advice and guidance – who is there for me, from epic chat sessions to life advice, always with the kindest heart. Thank you so much, lovely, for everything you do. You make everything better. Also, thank you for insisting that, no matter what changes we made, Oswin's cousin Osmeralda had to stay in!

To the genius Sarah Warburton, for bringing the world of Starfell so vividly to life – I still get goose bumps every time your illustrations start coming in and cannot tell you how proud I am to work with you – thank you so much.

Thank you also to Tuppence Middleton, for the absolutely incredible audio recordings of Starfell! Of course, with such a delightfully Starfell-y name, I had to give the fiercest Howling aunt your name, in honour.

Huge thanks to Sean Williams for the incredible cover, Elorine Grant for the beautiful text design and layout, and a massive thank-you to everyone at HarperCollins for their warmth and brilliance. A special thank-you to Ann-Janine Murtagh, Jo-Anna

Parkinson, Louisa Sheridan, Jessica Dean, Alex Cowan and Beth Maher.

Thank you so much to all the wonderful booksellers, teachers and librarians – true superheroes of this past year!

But the biggest thank you is to you – the reader. Thank you so much for buying a copy of Starfell (or borrowing it from your library!), and to everyone who has shared their love – who sent through pictures of themselves dressed up on World Book Day (all the Oswins!), who've drawn pictures of their favourite characters – you have all made this author so very happy. I really hope you enjoy the next book!

Read on for a glimpse of the next book in the Starfell series . . .

STARFELL

Willow Moss and the Magic Thief

Unexpected Tidings

As they entered a small village with rolling green hills and sheep grazing in the distance, Essential set the broom to 'SUNDAY STROLL' so they could recover from their somewhat uncomfortable journey.

But, as they slowed down, Willow noticed that scattered here and there were large black patches scarring the hillsides.

'That's odd, I wonder what those are?' she asked, pointing.

Essential turned to look, but, before she could reply, they heard a loud cawing overhead, and Willow saw a raven circling above. Its wings glittered like it was dusted with gold.

'Oh!' said Essential. 'It's the raven Pimpernell uses for the post – I'd recognise that glitter anywhere. She must have sent it after us with a note.'

They flew to meet the bird, who perched on the end of the long broomstick handle, allowing Essential to take the letter from its claws.

'Thanks, Frank,' said Essential, and the raven flew away.

Then she frowned at the letter she'd opened. 'It's from Rubix – Pimpernell will have sent it on. It must be important.'

Rubix Grimoire, Essential's guardian, was also the editor of the *Grimoire Gazette* and a senior member of the Enchancil. Willow knew it was possible she would have news of Silas.

'What does it say?' asked Willow anxiously.

'Read it for yourself – she's addressed it to you too.'

Dearest Essential and Willow,

I hope that things with Pimpernell are going smoothly. Here are the headlines from me.

The Howling sisters – the aunts of Willow's elvish friend, Twist – came to visit last week. We got into a dispute when I suggested the elves need to arrange a truce with the trolls so that we can all work together to fight Silas. They made it rain inside my house at the idea. Tensions between the two communities are at an all-time high since part of Troll Country was taken up by the ancient elvish kingdom that reappeared from underground. Technically, this means it was always there, but the trolls aren't seeing it that way at all. (They're attempting to take land from Dwarf Territory to make up for the loss – though, of course, they try that every year. The dwarfs aren't having it.)

Willow winced at this, considering she was the one who'd brought the kingdom of Llandunia back. It made the hard knot of guilt inside her grow to know the trolls, elves and dwarfs were fighting because of it. She kept reading.

Ultimately, despite their frustration, the elves have now assured the Enchancil they will work as a team with the trolls. This is in part due to the fact that Celestine Bear has agreed that elves can have a seat at the Enchancil again for the first time in fifty years.

This hasn't been received well by all – the elves, as you know, are not known for their tact when they think an idea is stupid. Not to mention that some are afraid that they will use their weather abilities to fry people with lightning again. The Howling sisters have sworn to rein in their tempers. This is good advice for us all. Now the threat that Silas poses to us all has been exposed, it is more important than ever for magical folk to be united. We are hopeful that troll chief Megrat and dwarf king Zazie may come to a peace agreement.

The Enchancil is also working with the broommakers, the Mementons, to ensure that all magical people have some form of quick transportation in case a militant band of the Brothers of Wol start rounding up more witches and wizards.

As you may have heard, after Silas was captured, some of the Brothers were released from the Gerful chalk he had been using to control them. A few, on realising what had happened, were grateful to the magical community for setting them free and have begun working with the Enchancil – but, alas, most of them refused to believe that magical folk could ever be trusted and remain loyal to their missing leader. We are still trying to reason with them, but, as they have once again taken refuge in the fortress of Wolkana, which is impenetrable to all magic, it is difficult to establish a line of communication. Each time we try, they attack our envoys with flaming arrows.

No news of Silas as yet. Hopefully, the rock dragons are proving too strong for him.

'I'm glad some of the Brothers of Wol have started to work with the Enchancil,' observed Essential, pushing up her glasses. 'I just wish the rest would see sense.'

'When it comes ter magic, those cumberworlds 'aven't seen sense fer eleventy-billy-bob years. Not sures why they'd try bovvering wiff it now,' said Oswin.

'It's good news that even *some* of them have seen the truth,' Willow said, and they kept reading Rubix's letter.

The only other news is a bit closer to home. For some reason, the entire area around the Midnight Market has gone under permanent darkness. My own house, just a mile away, is perfectly fine – the sun is still rising and setting as it always has. It must be some sort of rogue magic? Perhaps one of the stall-holders did something to encourage the market's nefarious reputation.

Speaking of strange, nefarious things, I ran into Amora Spell the other night. I know she used to be your granny's potions partner, Willow. She's returned to her potions stall, though it has undergone some transformations! I must admit I was never much of a fan of hers, but as she was a family friend I thought you might be interested to know that she's back. I must say I always thought she was a bit of a fraud, but perhaps I was wrong, as I've never seen her stall so busy or popular, and full of such new and exciting potions. Thought you might want to know, Willow, as I am aware you were looking for a cure for your stolen magic. Maybe she can help? Anyway, must get on with the latest edition of the *Grimoire Gazette* – the gist of which I've shared with you already, so at least you're the first to hear.

Stay safe and stay out of trouble.

With love,

Rubix Grimoire

When Willow got to the end of the letter, she cried out in excitement. 'Amora Spell – Rubix has found her!'

Clearly, Willow's mother hadn't told Rubix *everything*, or she would have known that her granny's old partner was a fraud and a cheat, and that Rubix was spot on about there being something very iffy about her.

Oswin snatched the letter and read the last paragraph himself, turning blood orange in the process. **'Not 'ard ter guess why she's suddenlies so popular.'**

'I know!' said Willow, who – to both Essential and Oswin's surprise – looked delighted by this turn of events.

Smoke began to furl off the top of Oswin's head. **'Stall fulls o' new potions – yew know 'ow she suddenlies got that, right? She's using the Flossy Mistress's old potion notebook!'**

Willow nodded.

'An' yew is 'appy abouts this?' asked Oswin, raising his eyebrows.

Willow shook her head. 'Not happy about her being a fraud, a liar and a cheat, *no*, but I am happy, yes, because now we know where to find her.'

Oswin sighed. **'Oh, me greedy aunt, I should 'ave knowns yew wos gonna say that.'**

Willow looked at Essential. 'I know it specifically says to stay safe and stay out of trouble . . .'

Essential cocked her head. 'But you want to do the opposite?'

'Pretty much, yes.'

They grinned at each other.

'Fair enough,' said Essential, lips twitching. She glanced at her list of patients. 'Norman Verbena still has bubbles coming out of his mouth. I've told him time and again that the solution is to stop taking anti-balding potion, but he never listens. I think he can suffer the consequences a little longer, don't you?'

Willow's grin widened.

Essential put the list in her pocket. 'Let's prise that notebook from the hands of that—'

'Harpy-hag,' suggested Oswin.

'Harpy-hag,' Essential confirmed.

Willow smiled. 'Sounds like a plan.'

To be continued . . .

Read more inside . . .

Discover where Willow's story begins . . .

Willow Moss, the youngest and least powerful sister in a family of witches, has a magical ability for finding lost things – like keys, or socks, or wooden teeth. Useful, but not exactly exciting . . . Until the most powerful witch in the world of Starfell turns up at Willow's door and asks for her help.

A whole day – last Tuesday to be precise – has gone missing. And, without it, the whole universe could unravel. Now Willow holds the fate of Starfell in her rather unremarkable hands . . . Can she save the day – by finding the lost one?

Follow Willow's journey . . .

The magic is rising...

STARFELL

Willow Moss and the Forgotten Tale

DOMINIQUE VALENTE

Illustrated by SARAH WARBURTON

Willow Moss is a young witch with the power to find anything that has been lost. Her magic once helped her to save the world, but now it's misbehaving . . .

Worse still, Willow's friend Nolin Sometimes has just sent an urgent letter, asking for her help. He has seen ten minutes into the future – just enough time to discover that he's about to be kidnapped.

Willow is determined to find him, and her search takes her and her friends to the very edges of Starfell . . . and straight into danger.

With the darkest forces against her, and her own powers out of control, can Willow save her friend?